TRAPPER'S BLOOD

Locked together, Nate and the half-breed exerted their sinews to the utmost. Nate blocked a knee to the groin and countered with a head butt to the jaw, which rocked Santiago backward. But instead of weakening, Santiago roared like a berserk grizzly, opened his mouth wide, and swooped his gleaming teeth at Nate's throat.

In the nick of time Nate jerked his head to one side. The breed's short teeth sheared into the fleshy part of his shoulder instead of the soft tissue of his neck. Excruciating anguish rippled down his body. Blood splattered his skin. Nate threw himself backward to break Santiago's grip and nearly cried out when his shoulder was torn open.

Santiago reared up, a patch of buckskin and a flap of skin hanging from his bloody lips. He spat them out, bent back his head, and howled like a demented coyote.

Nate drove his forehead into the breed's gut. It was like slamming into a wall. His blow had no effect on Santiago, but it did make Nate's senses spin.

Venting a howl of savage glee, Santiago stabbed downward....

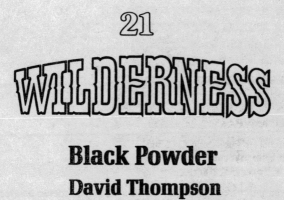

21

WILDERNESS

Black Powder
David Thompson

LEISURE BOOKS NEW YORK CITY

Dedicated to Judy, Joshua, and Shane,
the best family any man ever had.
And to Larry Bissonette,
for being a great guy.

A LEISURE BOOK®

July 1995

Published by

Dorchester Publishing Co., Inc.
276 Fifth Avenue
New York, NY 10001

Printed in the United States of America.

Chapter One

Simon Ward smiled as he set eyes on the dark green foothills of the majestic Rocky Mountains for the very first time in his life. "At last!" he exclaimed, rising in the stirrups to survey the broad sweep of stark peaks to the west. "At long, long last."

The petite young woman beside him smiled too, but her smile was not as wide, not as heartfelt. She hid that fact from her husband of only eighteen months by declaring, "They are beautiful, aren't they?"

"They're everything I told you they would be," Simon boasted. His saddle creaked as he sat back down and turned to put a hand on her slender shoulder. "Now do you see why I wanted us to come? Take a good look, Felicity. Anything we want is ours for the taking."

Felicity Ward placed her own hand on his. "I wouldn't go that far, dearest," she chided. "Other set-

5

tlers live in the mountains. And there are always the Indians." As she said that last word, she gazed rather fearfully off across the great expanse of prairie they had spent many weeks crossing.

"Sure there are settlers," Simon said, not noticing her timid glance in all his excitement, "but they're few and far between. As for the Indians—" He dismissed them with a gesture. "We didn't see hide nor hair of one red devil the whole trip, did we? If you ask me, all those awful stories we heard were tall tales meant to frighten children."

Felicity patted his hand. "I suppose." But what she really wanted to say was that the thought of running into Indians scared her half witless. She had spent their whole journey in a constant state of dread. Her nerves, which had never been very strong, were about worn to a frazzle.

Truth to tell, Felicity would much rather have been back in Boston than in the middle of the godforsaken wilderness. She'd never realized how good she'd had it until after her husband talked her into their bold venture.

Simon lifted his reins and clucked to his bay. "Come on, my love. Let's go find us a nice cool spot under some trees to take our midday rest." He tugged on the lead rope to their two pack animals and headed out.

Trying not to be obvious about it, Simon looked over a shoulder. For most of the morning he had been bothered by an uneasy feeling that they were being watched. Yet not once had he glimpsed anyone lurking on their back trail. He figured that he was simply being childish, letting his imagination get the better of him.

With a shrug, Simon cast the troublesome notion aside. He was not going to let anything spoil his good mood. His dream was coming true and he wanted to savor every moment.

The seed had been planted in his mind over a year ago. He had stopped at his favorite tavern on the way home from his job on the docks of Boston Harbor. He had planned to down a single cold ale and then head on home to his beloved.

But there had been a newcomer at the tavern, a cousin of the owner. And lo and behold, the man had been a genuine mountain man. He had sat there in his buckskin shirt and leggings and beaver hat, and he'd regaled them for hours with stories of his wild and woolly escapades in the Rockies.

It had fired up Simon's soul as nothing else in his life ever had. Except for Felicity, of course. He had taken to spending every spare moment daydreaming about the wonderful life they could build for themselves. Acres and acres of land, a fine cabin and whatever else they wanted were theirs for the taking.

By asking around, Simon had learned more about the vast frontier which stretched between the Mississippi River and the Pacific Ocean. He'd heard that a few hardy pioneers were already there. For the most part, though, the only whites within hundreds of miles were trappers, or mountain men, as the folks back in the States liked to call them.

It was wide open country, where a man could dig in roots, grow, and prosper. Where a family could be raised as a man saw fit. Where a man was accountable to no one other than himself and his Maker. It was where he yearned to live.

Simon had figured his wife would balk when he mentioned his brainstorm. She had been taken aback, but she had agreed after only a few talks. And so the chain of events had been set in motion.

As they made their way toward the slopes of the

low foothills, Simon again had that eerie feeling of being spied on. He shifted and scoured the rippling sea of high grass. Far to the northeast a small herd of shaggy buffalo grazed. To the southeast antelope were bounding off in long, graceful leaps. It was the same sort of tranquil scene he had seen many times. He did wonder why the antelope were fleeing, and then decided they had probably been spooked by a snake or some such.

"Is something wrong, Simon?"

Simon snapped around and plastered a grin on his face. "Heck, no. What makes you say that? I was just watching those antelope. They must be about the fastest creatures on four legs."

"Too bad that you couldn't get a shot at one. People say they make good eating."

It annoyed Simon to be reminded of his sole failure. He looked down at the trusty new Hawken, which rested across his thighs. Before leaving St. Louis, he had purchased it at the shop of two brothers by the same name, and he'd also bought a pair of flintlock pistols and a big butcher knife. When he'd strolled out of that place, he'd felt practically invincible.

On the long trek west, Simon had honed his skills with all three guns. At one time or another their supper pot had seen buffalo meat, black bear, deer, fox, prairie dog, grouse, quail, and once, elk. But he had never been able to sneak close enough to antelope to bring one down.

"I'll get one of them yet, you wait and see," Simon vowed. "And when I do, you can make a rug of its hide."

Felicity averted her face and scrunched up her nose. The idea of peeling off the skin of a bleeding animal with her own two hands, and then going to all the hard work of curing it, about made her ill. She would not let on, however. She knew that Simon was counting on her to do her fair share of the work. He had even bought a butcher knife just for her, which she kept rolled up in her bedroll.

A red hawk took wing above them and soared high into the crystal blue sky with a strident shriek.

"Look at that," Simon marveled. "These mountains are so full of game, all a man has to do is walk out his door and take his pick."

"There must be a lot of mountain lions and grizzly bears up there."

"A few," Simon admitted. "But none that we can't handle." He tried to sound more confident than he felt, for he had been told that grizzlies were to be avoided at all costs. They were described as ravenous monsters, bigger even than horses and as mean as sin, able to tear a man in half with a flick of a massive paw. The last thing he wanted was to tangle with one.

Simon bore to the right to skirt the base of the first hill, his eyes on the slope for a likely spot to rest. Suddenly the bay pricked its ears and snorted. Fearing a grizzly, Simon raised the Hawken and pressed his thumb to the hammer. Then he heard the unmistakable light tinkle of running water.

"A stream!" Simon exclaimed. He slapped his legs and urged the pack horses on. In under twenty yards he came upon the bank of a narrow ribbon of rushing water which had been hidden by the tall grass. It wound out from between a pair of hills and made off across the plain.

"Will you look at this!" Simon said. "We must have been close enough to hit it with a rock for the past ten miles, and we didn't even know it was there."

"Let's follow it. Maybe we'll find a pool." Felicity

took the lead. "It's been ages since I had a bath."

The mental picture of his wife stark naked brought a lump of raw passion to Simon's throat. While it was improper to admit as much, he lusted after her with an inhuman hunger. The minister of their church back in Massachusetts would never approve. But Simon couldn't help himself. From the moment their lips first touched, he had loved Felicity Morganstern more than life itself.

They climbed as the stream did and presently came to a wide bench lined by spruce trees to the west, boulders to the north, and a small but deep pool to the south.

Felicity squealed in delight and trotted to the water's edge. Sliding down, she cupped the cold water and took a thirsty sip. "Oh, Simon. It's simply delicious. Come and drink."

Dismounting, Simon had the presence of mind to walk to the nearest trees and loop his reins and the lead rope to a limb. All the way west, he had made it a point to always picket their horses when they stopped, no matter how briefly. He had been warned by men who knew that the loss of their animals could cost them their lives.

The pool had to be five feet deep, yet it was as clear as glass. For that matter, the air itself was invigorating. It had a crispness about it that Simon had not noticed before. He stooped down and drank his fill. Sitting back, he wiped his mouth with the back of his hand and glanced at his wife, who was grinning at him. "What?"

"You just look so darned adorable sometimes."

Simon didn't see how he could. His hair was a matted mess and hung down to his shoulders. His chin had sprouted stubble which might grow into a real beard in five or six weeks. He'd not bathed regularly in more days than he cared to count. And his wool shirt and pants were about worn at the seams. He needed a bath every bit as much as she did.

No, that was not quite true, Simon mused. Somehow, Felicity always managed to look as fresh as a daisy. She always smelled like one, too. Even when they had been in the saddle from dawn to dusk, riding under a blistering sun and beset by dust and insects, by some miracle she had been able to make herself presentable in no time at all once they made camp. It was a unique knack women had, he figured, one of those mysteries of the opposite sex that men were never privileged to know.

At the moment his wonderful wife was staring at the pool as if she had stumbled on a gold mine. "Do you really think it's all right for me to take a bath?"

"Why not? There isn't another living soul within two hundred miles of us. And the stream will flush the pool clean in no time." Simon rose. "Let me fill the water skins and the coffeepot and you can have at it."

Felicity clasped her hands together like a little girl given the present of her heart's desire. "Oh, my! To be clean again! To be able to comb my hair without wrestling it to death."

Chuckling, Simon took her horse over to the others. He stripped off their saddles and the packs and arranged them close to the pool so he could watch her bathe.

Just about then the bay lifted its head again, stared toward the rim of the bench, and nickered.

Simon paused in the act of dipping the cooking pot into the pool. He had learned to trust the bay's instincts, so he knew there had to be something out there, maybe the same thing that had been shadowing them the better part of the day. An animal, more than likely, he told himself. Several times on their long trip they had been followed by curious coyotes and wolves.

Still, Simon wanted to be sure. "The pool is yours," he announced. "I'll be right back." Grabbing the Hawken, he cradled it in his left arm and headed for the rim.

"Are you sure everything is all right?" Felicity asked.

"I give you my word," Simon said without thinking.

Grass swished about Simon's boots as he walked. A large butterfly fluttered past him. He pivoted to watch its aerial antics and saw his wife shedding her dress. His mouth went dry at the sight of her underclothes and the swell of her bosom. With an effort he tore his eyes away from her and went on.

The immense plain shimmered in the brilliant sunshine. Simon could see more buffalo than before. To the north, at the tree line, he spied several large forms moving among the pines. At first he thought they were deer, but on closer look he realized they were elk. His mouth watered at the prospect of a thick steak.

Nothing else stirred within the range of the young man's vision. He grinned at his foolish worries, hefted the Hawken, and ambled back toward their camp. It occurred to him that his wife might want to bathe in private. She was touchy about things like that.

Simon respected her for her modesty. She was every inch a lady, and he would not hesitate to slug anyone who implied otherwise. Felicity knew how he felt. She laughed at him sometimes, saying that it was silly of him to put her on some kind of pedestal.

Women just didn't understand men, Simon reasoned. When a man loved a woman, really and truly loved her, then that woman became the focus of his whole life. He would do anything for her, give her whatever she wanted if he had the means. More than that, he showed his devotion by always treating her with the utmost respect. If that was putting someone on a pedestal, then so be it.

Simon spotted his wife's dress lying beside the pool. There was no sign of her in the water, so he figured she had gone off into the spruce trees. Halting near their saddles, he waited for her to reappear. A minute went by. Then several more. He fidgeted and called out, "Darling, what's the matter? Did you snag your petticoat on a bush?"

There was no answer.

Becoming mildly alarmed, Simon cupped a hand to his mouth and bellowed, "Felicity! Where are you?"

Once more there was no reply.

A sensation of pure terror came over Simon as he abruptly dashed to the forest and called his wife's name several more times. When she did not respond, he darted madly among the trunks, seeking some sign of her. Ten minutes later, too bewildered to think straight, he returned to the pool.

In a daze, Simon picked up her dress and ran his fingers over the fabric. The horrible truth hit him then with the force of a physical blow and his knees buckled. His wife was gone! Somehow, something or someone had snatched her right out from under his nose!

Simon Ward tossed back his head and howled the name of the woman he loved.

Chapter Two

Nathaniel King was on the trail of five elk he had been tracking for the better part of two days when he heard a strange wail. Instantly he reined up his black stallion and sat listening for the sound to be repeated. It had been a human cry, yet one filled with more misery than any human voice should have to convey.

A free trapper by trade, Nate wore beaded buckskins and moccasins made for him by his Shoshone wife. A mane of black hair framed a rugged face bronzed by the sun and hardened by the elements. He carried a Hawken and had a brace of pistols around his waist. Slanted across his chest were a powder horn, ammo pouch and possibles bag. Eyes the color of emeralds studied the foothills to the south as he waited for the cry to be repeated so he could pinpoint where it came from.

Whoever had made it was plainly in some sort of

trouble. Whether white or Indian didn't matter to him. While some trappers ranked Indians as filthy savages, Nate knew better. They were people, plain and simple.

The strapping mountaineer had lived among them for a third of his life; the Shoshones had even formally adopted him into the tribe. In many ways he was more Indian than white, and he felt no shame admitting that fact.

Now, on hearing another cry, Nate jabbed his heels into the stallion's flanks and veered southward. He picked his way with care through the forest, his senses primed. It just might be that he had stumbled on a war party of Blackfeet or Piegans or some other hostile tribe.

Nate had been over this particular stretch of country before. He remembered the lay of the land well. On cresting a rocky spine, he spied a small stream below. It brought to mind the night many months ago when he had camped beside a pool on a wide bench just a little ways to the east. That was where the wail arose. He was sure.

Swinging to the west, Nate approached the bench in a wide loop. He slowed when he glimpsed four horses standing near the trees. All four were staring toward the pool. He looked, but did not notice anything out of the ordinary at first.

Then Nate heard an odd noise. It took him a few moments to identify it. Someone was crying, bawling like a baby. Even more surprising, he could tell it was a man. He moved closer and saw a figure on his knees close to the water.

The bawler had his arms clasped to his belly as if his innards were on fire. In front of him lay a garment of some kind.

Wary of a trick, Nate slowly walked the stallion to

the end of the pines and regarded the man closely. Right away he recognized a greenhorn. The store-bought clothes were a dead giveaway, as were the uncomfortable high-heeled city boots no trapper in his right mind would wear.

Squaring his broad shoulders, Nate nudged the stallion forward. The man was making so much noise, he never heard. A few yards shy of the camp, Nate drew rein and said quietly so as not to startle him, "Are you in pain, mister?"

Simon Ward had been so overcome by despair at being unable to find his wife that he had started crying before he could stop himself.

The young man from Boston had lived in secret horror of this very thing happening ever since they had left the last settlement way back in Missouri. Despite all his bluster to the contrary, Simon had not had much confidence in his ability to protect his wife. For one thing, he was not much of a woodsman. He had managed to keep the supper pot full every night only because game on the prairie had been so plentiful.

For another thing, Simon had never killed a human being and had no idea whether he could. The old-timers he had talked to in St. Louis and elsewhere had impressed on him that sooner or later he would have to do so. Any man who made his home in the mountains, they had claimed, was bound to run up against hostiles eventually. It was as inevitable as the rising of the sun. And where hostiles were concerned there was only one rule; kill or be killed.

Simon had not let Felicity know of his worry. He had not wanted her to think that he could not protect her if the need arose.

Now, to have the love of his life vanish without a

trace, virtually paralyzed him. Racked by intense guilt, Simon cried and cried even though he knew that he should get to his feet and go search for her. He just couldn't seem to stop himself.

But that had always been the case. Ever since he was a small boy, Simon had reacted to every undue hardship by bawling his brains out. His own brothers and sisters had branded him a bawl-baby. And while he did not do it as often as he once did, and certainly never where others, especially Felicity, could see him, he still had his moments.

Then someone spoke. Shocked to his core, Simon glanced up. His tears were choked off by his amazement at beholding a huge man who looked to be part Indian mounted on the biggest, blackest horse he had ever set eyes on. They almost seemed unreal to him, phantasms of his tormented mind.

"Are you in pain?" Nate King repeated, not knowing what to make of the greenhorn's expression. He looked at the garment, realized what it was, and scanned the area, alarmed. "Is there a woman with you?"

The reminder jolted Simon like a bolt out of the blue. Surging to his feet, he trained his rifle on the stranger and demanded, "Where is she, damn you? What have you done with her, you miserable heathen?"

The greenhorn was close to snapping. Any man could tell. Nate mustered a friendly smile and said, "Sheathe your claws, pilgrim. I'm a white-eye, like you. I haven't done anything to anyone. I heard you cry out and figured I could be of help, is all."

"You're white?" Simon said suspiciously. He had never seen a white man so dark of skin before, not even the mountain men he'd met in St. Louis. And he noticed that this one wore an eagle feather in his hair, jutting downward at the back.

Nate ignored the implication and pointed at the dress. "Listen, greener. If you don't need me, that's fine by this hos. But if your woman is in trouble, it wouldn't pay to be too proud. Savvy?"

Simon glanced down at his feet where Felicity's garment had fallen. "Oh, God! My wife," he said, fighting back a rising wave of more tears. His mind in a whirl, he swayed.

Thinking that the younger man was about to pass out on him, Nate dismounted. "Where is she?"

"I don't know," Simon said forlornly. "One minute she was right here, about to take a bath. The next she was gone." He motioned helplessly at the woods. "A grizzly must have dragged her off when I had my back turned."

"You would have heard it if one did," Nate said, turning his attention to the ground bordering the pool. "A griz likes to roar when it charges. Half scares most critters to death and makes them easy prey."

"Really?" Simon said, running his sleeve under his nose. He was still leery, but it appeared to him as if the newcomer was sincere about lending a hand, and he could use all the help he could get.

"Your wife never cried out?"

"No, sir. Not a peep." Simon indicated the rim. "I was over there, you see. My horse had acted up and I thought an animal might be nearby—" He stopped short when the stranger abruptly squatted to examine a strip of bare earth.

"It was no animal."

"What? How do you know?"

"Look here," Nate said, pointing. It had been his experience that most pilgrims could not track a bull buffalo through fresh mud, and he wanted the younger man to see for himself.

18

Simon stared but saw nothing except the earth. There were a few smudge and scratch marks with no rhyme or reason to them that he could discern. "Look at what, mister?"

Sighing, Nate responded, "Step around behind me and take a gander over my shoulder. I'll outline it with my finger."

Complying, Simon watched intently as the mountain man ran a fingernail along the outer edge of what appeared to be a half-moon scrape. "So?"

"It's the heel print of a man wearing moccasins," Nate revealed. "And this here"—he touched a shallow furrow that to the young Bostonian looked as if it had been made by a stick—"is where your wife dragged her foot trying to keep them from carrying her off."

"Them?" Simon repeated, his stomach churning as the full import of what the man was telling him sank home.

"There were two men, both wearing moccasins," Nate said as he moved along the edge of the pool to where the rushing water entered it. "One was a white man, the other a breed. They came out of those weeds on the other side of the stream, jumped it, and were on your wife before she knew they were there. One must have put a hand over her mouth and grabbed her around the shoulders while the other took hold of her around the legs. She struggled some, but it did her no good. They carried her back across and were long gone before you returned."

Flabbergasted, Simon gawked at this brawny wild man with the uncanny ability to read marks on the ground as if they were letters in a book. With this man's help, he just might be able to save Felicity.

Then it occurred to Simon Ward that maybe he was being too trusting. After all, he knew nothing about the stranger. And it was odd that the man should show up just minutes after his wife had been taken. For all he knew, the Good Samaritan might be in league with her abductors. Why, it might be, he mused, that this was no mountain man at all, but a common cutthroat.

Nate was bending to inspect prints near the stream when he noticed the greenhorn give him a mighty peculiar look, the same kind of look a person might give a ravenous wolf that had wandered into camp. Hoping to show the young man that there was no cause to distrust him, Nate straightened and offered his hand. "My manners aren't what they used to be. I'm Nate King. My family and I live in a cabin southwest of here a fair piece."

Simon automatically shook hands and marveled at the strength in King's grip. He suspected that the man could crush his fingers without hardly trying. "You have a family?"

"Sure do. My wife, Winona, is a Shoshone. We have a son named Zach and a little girl, Evelyn."

Simon believed the man was telling the truth. King's affection for his loved ones made his face light up like a candle. Simon relaxed a little, since in his estimation it was unlikely a genuine cutthroat would be a family man. "I'm Simon Ward. My wife's name is Felicity." That was all Simon intended to say, but he went on, unable to stop himself, the words rushing out of their own accord. "We came west to make a better life for ourselves, to live free as the birds, just as you and your family must do. It was my idea, you see. I talked Felicity into it. I told her everything would be fine, that no harm would come to her. I told her I'd protect her no matter what. And then she disappeared and I didn't know what had happened to her and I was at my wit's end so I—"

"Cried?" Nate finished when the younger man hesitated. The emotional outpouring had told him a lot, and none of it raised his opinion of the greenhorn.

Cut to the quick by the tone that the mountain man used, Simon blurted, "I couldn't help myself. If something really bad happens, I go all to pieces. My mother says I have a sensitive nature."

"What does your pa say?"

"That I'm an idiot."

Nate was inclined to agree with the father. He shook his head and moved on. All this was well and good, but they had a woman to find, and quickly, or the young fool might never see his wife again. "Saddle up. I'll scout around and be back in a few minutes."

Simon opened his mouth to voice a question, but King suddenly leaped across the stream and plunged into the vegetation on the other side. He had wanted to explain further, to let the mountain man know that he wasn't a whiner by nature, that he simply had the soul of a poet, as one of his teachers had put it. But it would have to wait, he reflected. King had a point. Felicity came first. He hastened to obey.

Nate glanced back once, then concentrated on the spoor. The men who had taken the woman were skilled. They had left few tracks, and probably would have left none at all had they not been burdened by their captive. Once over the rim of the bench and out of earshot, they had broken into a run. At one point the man in the lead, the white man, had slipped and gouged his knees into the soil. There was evidence of a brief scuffle. When the kidnappers went on, they ran side by side and the footprints of the white were much deeper than those of the breed.

It was not hard for Nate to determine what had happened. Felicity Ward had been fighting hard to break free every step of the way, and she had caused the white man in front to fall. The man had lost his grip. Felicity had then turned on her second captor, but before she could tear loose, the breed had knocked her out. The white man had then draped her over a shoulder and the pair had gone on.

At the bottom of the bench were hoofprints. Two horses had been ground-hitched there for quite some time. Both had urinated, one between its legs, the other behind them. That told Nate that one had been a stallion, the other a mare.

Having learned all he needed, Nate raced to the top of the bench. Ward had saddled a bay and another animal and was hard at work loading the packs.

"You have a decision to make," Nate announced.

Simon had been so engrossed in his chore that he had not heard the trapper approach. He started, and clutched at one of his pistols. "King! Damn! Don't creep up on me like that."

Nate did not waste a moment. "If we hurry, we might be able to catch them before they get very far. One of them is riding double." He nodded at the pack animals. "But we won't have a prayer if we're dragging them along. It would slow us down too much."

"You want me to leave the packhorses?" Simon said, aghast. All the worldly goods he and Felicity owned were on those two animals.

"And your wife's horse," Nate said. "She can ride back with you."

Simon was reluctant to do it. He feared that a wild beast might come along and kill the horses or spook them. Or a band of Indians might ride by and steal them. Without those animals, Felicity and he would not last long. But which was more important? he asked himself. His wife, or their personal effects?

"Give me a minute," he said, and led the three horses over to the pines.

Nate swung onto his stallion and waited by the stream. When the young man joined him, he forded and broke into a gallop. At the bottom he showed Ward the hoof tracks, then circled to pick up the trail.

"There's something I've been meaning to ask you," Simon mentioned as the mountain man rode bent low to the ground. "How do you know that one of these men is white and the other is a half-breed?"

Nate answered without looking up. "Most white men walk with their toes pointed out and take long strides. Indians, by and large, walk with their toes bent in and take smaller steps."

"So you're saying that it's plain one of them is white. That I can understand. But how can you tell the other is a breed? I mean, if the toes are bent in, maybe it's a full-blooded Indian."

"No," Nate said, rising. He had found where the tracks led away from the bench, bearing due south. "The second man's toes are only partly bent in, and he takes long steps."

"Oh."

They sped on, Nate in the lead, winding among the pines at a reckless pace. Simon Ward was awed by the mountain man's riding ability. It was as if the man and the black stallion were one. He was hard pressed to keep up but resolved not to fall behind. Not when his wife's life was at stake. Or worse.

The idea jarred Simon. Until that moment he had not given much thought to what Felicity's abductors planned to do with her. Yet it was doubtful they had taken her just to kill her. A burning rage flared in him as he pictured her being abused.

"Watch out!" Nate King cried.

Simon blinked and looked up to see a low limb sweeping toward him. At the very last instant he ducked under it and was spared. He saw King shake his head and wished he would quit making a jackass of himself. He wanted to earn the mountain man's respect, not his contempt.

If the young Bostonian had been able to read Nate's mind, he would have been even more upset. Nate was convinced that Ward had no business whatsoever being in the Rockies. The wilderness was no place for amateurs. Time and again he had run into people like Ward, folks whose daydreams eclipsed their common sense, whose hankering for living on the frontier flew in the face of their inability to fend for themselves.

Nature was a hard taskmaster. There was one unwritten law, and one only, by which the many wild creatures lived; survival of the fittest. Humans were not accorded any special treatment. When they were out of their element, they had to deal with Nature on its own terms. Which meant they were fair game for any prowling grizzly, painter or hostile.

People like the Wards did not last long. They needed plenty of time to learn how to live off the land, and time was one luxury few ever had. There were simply too many dangers.

Nate's reflection ended when the pines thinned. The next several hills were virtually barren. He scanned them for a glimpse of the kidnappers, but they were nowhere to be seen. Slowing, he leaned to the right to better study the tracks. A dozen yards further on the trail changed direction. The two men had angled to the southwest into dense woodland.

"Why have you slowed down?" Simon asked, drawing abreast of the stallion.

"Either these vermin know that we're after them

or they're just being canny," Nate said. He was about to pick up the pace when his keen eyes spotted a small object lying near the trail. Drawing rein, he slid down and picked it up.

"What do you have there, Mister King?"

"Call me Nate." Nate sniffed it, then held it up for Ward to examine.

"Why, that's part of a cigarette, isn't it?"

Nate had thought so too, at first glance. But it wasn't the hand-rolled variety of smoke favored by some of the trapping fraternity. "This is a *cigarrillo*. A Spanish brand. I saw a lot of folks using them when I took my family to New Mexico some time ago."

"But what would a Spanish cigarette be doing here? Do you think the men we're after are Mexicans?"

"No," Nate said, and let it go at that. The *cigarrillo* was a disturbing clue, one he would rather not share until he was certain. He prayed that he was wrong as he stepped into the stirrups and pressed on.

The spacing and depth of the tracks showed that the kidnappers were moving at a faster clip. The trail climbed to the top of a ridge, stuck to the crest for half a mile, and went down the other side. Either by luck or design the kidnappers had come on a game trail and taken it south to make better time.

For the next hour Nate and Simon pushed their mounts to the limit. A few miles to the west reared the regal Rockies, while to the east rippled the endless ocean of grass.

The trail crossed yet another hill, and as they reached the boulder-strewn crest, Nate abruptly reined up.

"What is it this time?" Simon inquired as the trapper slid to the ground.

David Thompson

"They stopped at this spot for a short while."

"To rest their horses?"

Hunkering, Nate probed for telltale signs. Blades of grass had been pressed flat, as if by the weight of a body. Broken stems testified to a brief scuffle. "They tied up your wife. She must have come around and tried to get away. See these footprints? The breed held her while the white man did the tying."

"May their souls rot in hell!" Simon said.

"Count your blessings," Nate responded, stepping to his mount.

"How do you mean?"

"She's still alive, isn't she? And they haven't tried to force themselves on her. Yet." Nate saw the young man blanche, but he did not regret being so blunt. Someone should have been equally blunt long before the Wards left Boston. It would have spared them both a heap of misery.

For the better part of two hours the free trapper and the Bostonian forged southward. At length they came to a wide clearing where there was evidence that many men had encamped for many days. There were so many tracks, all in a jumble, that it took Nate a while to sort them out. When he had, he frowned and gazed to the southeast, the direction their quarry had taken.

"Why so glum?" Simon wondered. "They're not that far ahead of us now, are they?"

"About an hour."

"Then we have the bastards!" Simon exclaimed. As an afterthought, he added, "How many of them are there, by the way?"

"I counted fourteen, but that's not the worst of it." Nate faced him.

The news was disheartening to Simon. Two against fourteen were bad odds. "What can possibly be worse?" he snorted.

"Your wife is in the clutches of slavers."

Chapter Three

Slavers! The very word was enough to bring goose-bumps to the flesh of every woman living in the mountains, red or white. They knew that if they were to fall into the hands of the coldhearted rogues, they would never see those they most cared for again.

No one knew exactly how many women had been stolen over the past decade or so. The total bandied about by the trapping community stood at seventy, or better.

It was widely known that the slavers had taken women from eight or nine different tribes as well as white settlers. There was an unconfirmed rumor that a few blacks, females *and* males, had also fallen prey. Some of the hapless victims were sold to Comanches, who paid extremely well for white wives. Others were sold south of the border to wealthy Mexicans. The blacks, according to the rumor, were carted to the deep South and handed over to certain unscrupulous plantation owners.

Only once had the slavers been caught in the act, and that by a tribe of Sioux who had harried them for scores of miles before the slavers finally released the four maidens they had kidnapped.

All the other times the slavers got clean away.

Nate had thought that merely mentioning them by name would give Ward some notion of what they were up against. But he had overlooked the younger man's profound ignorance of frontier life.

"Slavers? Who are they? Are you telling me that they make slaves of the women they abduct?"

Motioning at a log that lay beside the charred remains of a camp fire, Nate straddled it and sat. "Have a seat, pilgrim. We need to palaver a spell and set you straight on a few things. It won't do to get into a racket with this bunch with you not knowing the facts."

Simon stayed right where he was, next to his bay. "We don't have time for this nonsense, King! Every second we dawdle is another second my precious wife is in peril! I say that we ride out this very moment."

Unfazed by the outburst, Nate tapped the log. "Sit, pronto. Unless you want me to fetch you over and plunk you down." If the situation had not been so deadly serious for Mrs. Ward, he would have laughed at the comical pout her husband wore as Simon did as he wanted. Emotionally, the man was about as mature as his son, which was downright pitiful.

"Now, first things first," Nate said after Simon was settled. "I don't take it kindly of you to keep giving me a hard time. I don't have to do this, you know. There's nothing to keep me from turning right around and heading for the Shoshone village."

"I thought that you claimed you live in a cabin,"

Simon said sullenly. He did not like being treated as if he were next to worthless, and he still did not trust the mountain man completely.

"We do about ten months of the year," Nate disclosed. "But in the summer my wife likes to spend a couple of moons with her kin. My wife and children are with them now. I was off elk hunting when I bumped into you."

"Oh."

"Now listen, and listen good." Nate leaned forward. "Slavers are the foulest, meanest sons of bitches on two legs. They'll kill anyone who gets in their way without a second thought. Do you understand? If you were to charge into their camp and demand to have your wife handed over, you'd be dead the moment after you got the words out of your mouth." He paused. "Unless, of course, the slavers were in a frolicsome mood. Then they'd likely carve you up a bit to hear you scream before they rubbed you out."

Simon figured that the frontiersman was exaggerating a little. He'd heard that mountain men were fond of spinning tall tales. "You make them sound as bad as heathen savages."

"Indians aren't savages," Nate said stiffly. "But in one sense, you're right. Slavers are worse than any Indian alive. I know, because at one time or another I've tangled with practically every kind of Indian there is, from Blackfeet to Bloods to Apaches."

"If they're so evil, why haven't they been arrested and put in prison?"

Nate could not stifle a guffaw. "Who is going to arrest them, pilgrim? In case it hasn't sunk in yet, there's no law out here. None at all. Once a man leaves the States, he's on his own."

Simon realized that he had made a stupid remark,

but he was so flustered by the nightmare that had beset his wife that his mind was clouded by anxiety. "So what do we do when we catch up with these cutthroats?"

"I'll get to that in a moment." Nate stared off across the plain. He, too, was impatient to get under way, but he had to make Ward see the light. "First you have to learn who these slavers are. Some are renegade whites who are wanted back in the States, others are Mexicans wanted in their country, while still others are outcast Indians and breeds. They're no account any way you lay your sights. And each and every one of them has a string of kills to his credit."

Simon shuddered. To think that his Felicity was in the clutches of such fiends! He wished now that he had never talked her into making the journey. He wished that he had left well enough alone and stayed in Boston where they belonged. What in the world had gotten into him?

"As for how we'll handle it," Nate went on, "it depends on what we find when we overtake them. If all goes well, we'll be able to rescue your missus without much of a fuss. If not—" He shrugged.

"What then?"

"Then we do what we have to. Now let's light a shuck while we still have some daylight left. And hope to high heaven that the slavers make camp and don't elect to keep on going through the night as they sometimes do when they suspect someone is dogging their heels."

It did not dawn on Simon until they had been in the saddle fifteen minutes that the trapper had a point about being treated unkindly. It was wrong of him to still be suspicious. King was putting his life in jeopardy for two complete strangers. If the slavers were everything the trapper claimed, then King had to know that he might wind up dead before too long. It gave Simon considerable food for thought.

The tracks led them down out of the foothills and onto the prairie. Simon tried not to dwell on the fact that each passing minute took them farther from the packhorses and Felicity's animal.

Presently twilight shrouded the landscape. Simon thought that maybe the mountain man would slow down, but King held to a steady trot.

The sunset was spectacular. Framed by the pristine peaks, the sky blazed red and orange and pink. Golden rays shot over the Rockies like shafts from heaven. Any other time, Simon would have been mesmerized. As it was, he looked, then looked away.

With nightfall rose a cool breeze. Simon would have given anything to be by a warm fire. To have his wife snuggled in his arms. He fantasized of doing just that, and so vivid was his fantasy that he didn't notice Nate King had stopped. Suddenly the black stallion was right there in front of him.

"Dear God!" Simon cried. He wrenched on the reins so hard, he snapped the bay's head around. It caused the horse to veer just enough to one side to miss the black stallion by a hand's width. Simon let out the breath he had not known he was holding. He pretended not to notice that Nate King was glaring at him.

"Yell again a little louder, why don't you, pilgrim? I don't reckon the slavers heard you the first time."

"We've caught up with them?" Simon asked, elation coursing through him at the prospect of soon being reunited with his wife.

"They're yonder a little ways," Nate said, nodding to the southeast. "We'll leave the horses here and go on foot. Try not to make much noise if you can help it."

The young Bostonian stared hard into the night but saw no sign of those they were after, not even the faint glow of a distant camp fire. Figuring that the slavers had made a cold camp, he slipped from the saddle, waited for the trapper to lead off, and dogged the frontiersman's footsteps.

On all sides, chest-high grass enclosed them. Nate King hunched low and glided forward, parting the stems with the barrel of his Hawken, his ears straining to hear more of the sounds he had heard a minute before. Other than a faint rustling of the grass, he made no noise at all.

Simon tried to do the same, but try as he might, he kept stepping on clumps that crackled underfoot. Or he would push against the grass in front of him a bit too hard and it would snap off. Once King glanced around. "Sorry," Simon whispered. "I'm doing the best I can."

Nate knew that. Which was why he did not find fault with the greenhorn, but went on, moving slowly in the belief that the slower they went, the less noise Ward was likely to make. It worked to some extent.

Simon was impatient to catch sight of his wife again. He expected to come on the slavers at any second. So when a minute went by, then two, then five, and more, he began to think that maybe the mountain man was wrong, that maybe they were chasing shadows. It angered him so much that he tapped King on the back and whispered testily, "Are you sure the slavers are camped nearby? If you ask me, we're wasting our damn time."

Nate stopped and turned. It galled him to have his judgment questioned by someone whose claim to sound judgment was almost laughable. Grabbing Ward by the front of his woolen shirt, Nate hoisted him erect and pointed. "Any more questions, mister?" he growled.

Fifty yards away were the dancing flames of a camp fire. Figures were seated around it. Others moved about in its vicinity.

Simon could hardly credit his own eyes. It stupefied him that the frontiersman had spotted the camp from so far off. And he was deeply ashamed for having doubted him. He nodded, and King let go. "What now?" he whispered.

"You stay put while I go have a look-see," Nate said. He expected an argument and was pleased when Ward merely bobbed his chin. Bending low, Nate padded forward on cat's feet. When he glimpsed the fire through the thick grass, he slowed to a snail's pace.

That the slavers had seen fit to make a fire was encouraging. It meant they had no notion that someone was after them. They were bound to post guards, but not until most of the band had turned in.

Nate strained to hear snatches of conversation. A pair of men were talking in Spanish. While he had learned a little of the language down in New Mexico, he did not know it well enough to be able to understand what they were saying. Others were chatting in English, but he was not quite close enough to eavesdrop.

A dozen yards from the camp, Nate shifted his pistols. Usually he wore them wedged under his belt on either side of his big metal buckle. Now he slid them around to his hips so they would not drag on the ground.

Easing onto his belly, Nate snaked nearer. He would crawl a foot or so, then pause to look and listen. In this cautious manner he drew within six feet of the flattened area in which the slavers had made their camp.

The grass had not only been bent flat, but wide areas had been grazed to the ground. In some spots the soil had been torn up, as if by a pick and shovel.

Nate recognized the handiwork of buffalo when he saw it. The slavers had gathered a pile of dry chips and were using the dung as fuel. Its dusky scent hung heavy in the air, mixed with the aroma of tobacco and the smell of horses.

As Nate had determined earlier in the day, there were fourteen cutthroats in the band. Eight were clustered at the fire, swapping stories. A few others played cards. One man was cleaning his rifle, another honed a butcher knife. Saddles and packs were lined up near the horse string for a quick getaway if need be.

It worried Nate that there was no trace of Felicity Ward. Given the vicious temperament of slavers, he would not put it past them to have slit her throat and dumped her body on the plain if she had given them too much trouble. Simon and he might have passed within a few yards of her cold corpse and never known it.

Then a lean slaver who wore a black *sombrero* and Mexican-style clothes rose from near the fire with a tin plate in his left hand and walked over to the saddles. The toe of his boot nudged what appeared to be a large bundle wrapped in a brown blanket, and the 'bundle' uncoiled and stiffly sat up.

It was a young woman. Felicity Ward. She was slight of frame and had sandy, disheveled hair. Her face was streaked with dirt, as were her underclothes, the only garments she had on.

"I brought you some food, senora," the slaver declared. "It is not much. Beans and dried beef. But it is all we have."

"I'm not hungry, Julio," Felicity said.

"*Por favor*, you must do as I say. You have no choice. Gregor says you are to eat if I have to force it down your throat."

"Tell that brute—" Felicity began, and froze when another slaver stood and came toward them.

This one was a huge man with the torso of a bear and a face scarred by many fights. Greasy brown hair hung down past his sloped shoulders, held in place by a coonskin cap. He wore grimy buckskins and carried four pistols in his belt. "Tell me what, woman?" he demanded in a gravelly voice.

Felicity was not given a chance to answer. The man called Gregor struck with lightning speed, lunging and slapping her across the cheek with a resounding crack. She crumpled, dazed, and Gregor seized her and shook her as a terrier might shake a rabbit.

"You still haven't gotten it through your thick skull, bitch! When we tell you to do something, you do it, no questions asked. You don't say no. You don't gripe. You don't insult us. You just do it!"

Gregor flung her down and jabbed a thick finger under her nose. "The next time you rile me, I'll strip you buck naked and drag you behind my horse for a mile or two. That ought to teach you to hold your tongue."

Spinning, Gregor shook a fist the size of a ham at the Mexican. "What the hell is the matter with you, Trijillo? I thought you're supposed to be one mean hombre? When a woman won't do what you want, slap her around some until she does. Don't ever let me hear you say 'please' again."

Julio's contempt was thick enough to be cut with

a knife. "My apologies, senor. But I am not used to treating women the way you do. Where I come from, a man does not go around beating on those who are weaker than him."

Gregor motioned in disgust. "Is that a fact? Well, you'll never make a good slaver then. A good beating is the only thing that keeps most of these cows in line." He started back to the fire, then paused. "I never should have let you join up. When we get back below the border, go find yourself another line of work."

The other slavers had not shown much interest in the exchange. One man, though, a beefy breed who wore only a breechcloth and knee-high moccasins, had picked up his rifle and held it as if ready to shoot should Gregor and the Mexican come to blows. He did not lower the gun until Gregor had rejoined the group around the fire.

Nate was mildly puzzled. The leader's brutality was typical of slavers, but Julio Trijillo's behavior had not been. The Mexican had acted genuinely concerned for the captive's welfare. He gathered that Trijillo was new to the slaving trade, perhaps a bandit who had thrown in with them not really knowing what he was letting himself in for.

Not that it mattered much. The other thirteen would as soon beat their captive silly as look at her.

Of immediate concern to Nate was how to get the woman out of there without being killed in the process. Nate studied the layout of the camp. He saw Mrs. Ward sit back up and morosely pick at her meal. She was the perfect picture of misery.

It made Nate think of his own wife, Winona, and how he would react if she were to suffer the same fate. He thanked God that she was safe and sound, many miles away in the Shoshone village.

At that moment, back in the grass, Simon Ward squatted on the balls of his feet and impatiently waited for the frontiersman to return. To stay there and not do anything, knowing that his wife was so close, was one of the hardest things Simon had ever had to do. Horrid images fired his brain, images of vile acts the slavers might be inflicting on her. He wanted to jump up and go charging into their camp. It took every ounce of self-control he had not to.

The wait stretched Simon's already frayed nerves to the breaking point. He was so overwrought that when a dark shape reared up in front of him, he whipped his rifle to his shoulder and started to pull back the hammer.

"It's me," Nate whispered, ready to grab the barrel and shove it aside if he heard a click. He'd rather not, though, since the gun might go off and alert the slavers. Fortunately, Ward lowered the Hawken.

"Did you see her?" Simon asked urgently.

"Yes."

"Has she been harmed?"

Most mountain men were shrewd judges of human nature. They had to be in order to survive. So Nate knew beyond a shadow of a doubt that if he told the truth, nothing he could say or do would stop Simon Ward from barrelling to Felicity's side without a thought for his own welfare, or anyone else's.

"She's fine," Nate fibbed. "Eating supper, the last I saw."

"They're feeding her?" Simon said in surprise, having assumed the fiends would half starve his beloved to death.

Nate sank to one knee. "Keep in mind that to them, the slave trade is a business. They can't get top dollar for their goods if the merchandise is damaged."

"Do we go get her now?"

"No, we wait until they've turned in."

Simon was none too happy. "Since she's my wife, I think I should have the greater say. And I vote that we rescue her right this minute. You can distract them somehow while I go in and whisk her out of there."

"Won't work," Nate said, sitting. "Even if I lured them off, they're not about to leave her unguarded. Four or five would stay put and gun you down the moment you showed yourself."

There was no denying the trapper's logic, but Simon still simmered at yet another delay. Bowing his head, he tried to shut thoughts of poor Felicity from his mind.

Unchecked bittersweet memories flooded through Simon: the first time they had met at the market where she worked, their first, fleeting kiss in the back of a buggy, their hectic wedding day, and the bliss of their wedding night.

Felicity was the only woman Simon had ever known in the Biblical sense. He'd always been so shy in that regard that it had taken him months to muster the nerve to hold her hand. It was safe to say that their wedding night had been the single greatest night of his entire life.

"Do you love your wife, Nate?" Simon asked.

The unexpected question made the mountain man glance up sharply. Having lived on the frontier for so long, where folks tended to mind their own business, he tended to forget that Easterners liked to pry into the personal affairs of others. "Yes, I do," he answered honestly. "She's my whole life."

"That's how I feel about Felicity. So you'll have to forgive me if I push too much. If anything should happen to her, I wouldn't want to live."

It sounded to Nate as if the younger man were

about to burst into tears again. To forestall that, he said, "I don't hold it against you. I was your age once."

Simon scrutinized the mountain man's features. "Not that long ago, I daresay. You don't appear to be that much older than I am."

"It's not how long a person lives, but how much living they do," Nate commented. "You're right, though. I was too young to know any better when I gave up an accounting career in New York City to come live with my uncle up in the mountains."

"Where is he now?"

Nate plucked at a blade of grass. "He died shortly after we got here."

"And you've been fending for yourself ever since?"

"A friend of my uncle's took me under his wing and taught me how to stay alive in the wild."

"Really? I wish I had someone to teach me."

Nate King offered no reply. But it set him to thinking that maybe he had treated the greenhorn too harshly, that maybe he should give Simon the same benefit of the doubt that Shakespeare McNair, his uncle's friend, had given him. Do unto others, as the Good Book put it.

Simon peered toward the camp, anxious to be off. "How long do you think it will be before the slavers fall asleep?"

Before Nate could respond, a wavering scream rent the night, the scream of a woman in mortal terror. He made a grab for the Bostonian, but he was a hair too slow.

Simon Ward was off like a shot, plowing through the grass to go save the woman he loved.

Chapter Four

Hours earlier and many miles to the northwest, Winona King had realized that she was being stalked when her pinto mare swung its head around, ears pricked toward the top of the rise they had just crossed.

The wife of the man known as Grizzly Killer was a credit to her people. She did not panic. She did not go into a bout of hysteria as some of her sisters from east of the Mississippi might have done. No, Winona King merely firmed her grip on her rifle and guided the mare behind a thicket so that she could spy on her back trail without being seen.

Winona was a Shoshone—-and proud of it. Her people were widely respected by their friends and widely feared by their enemies. Even the notorious Blackfeet, who raided at will over the northern mountains and plains, regarded the Shoshones as fierce fighters.

Black Powder

Since joining herself to Nate King as his woman, Winona had been in more than her share of tight situations. Her husband's wanderlust had taken her from the dry deserts of New Mexico to the sandy shores of the Great Water far, far to the west. In her travels she had met many who wanted to deprive her of her life, and she was still around.

Winona had no idea who was after her this time. Early that morning she had left her children in the care of her aunt and gone off to hunt. She wanted to surprise her man with a new buckskin shirt when he came back from elk hunting. To do that, she needed a fresh hide.

So for most of the morning Winona had sought fresh deer sign, and on finding it she had followed the tracks to the southeast.

Now it was late afternoon. A short while ago, while crossing a tableland, Winona had idly glanced back and thought she saw a wisp of dust possibly raised by another rider. She had reined up and waited to see if anyone appeared. When no one had, she'd gone on.

Then the pinto looked around, and Winona knew beyond a shadow of doubt that she had someone on her trail. Her guess was that it might be a war party of Blackfeet, or of any other tribe with whom the Shoshones were at perpetual war.

Quite often enemies were content to steal horses, or women. Winona had lost a number of close friends and relatives to marauding bands, and she did not care to share their fate.

She was not very worried. Her mare had superb stamina. It could hold its own against most any horse. In addition, she had the rifle her husband had bought for her and taught her to shoot, plus a pair of pistols and a knife.

Nate always insisted that she be well armed when she ventured anywhere. It amused some of the other Shoshone women to see her go around armed like a warrior, but Winona ignored them. Her husband was right. It was fitting that a woman hold her own in all aspects of married life, which included being able to protect herself and her family as well as any man.

Winona rested her rifle across her thighs and scanned the terrain she had traversed. Nothing moved, not so much as a chipmunk. That in itself was ominous.

A gust of wind stirred the raven tresses that cascaded down to the small of Winona's back. She had on a beaded buckskin dress and short moccasins. Around her slim waist was a red sash Nate had bought for her at the last rendezvous. She had protested, saying it was a waste of money. But he had seen the gleam in her eyes when she saw it. And, as always, all she had to do was show an interest in something and he did whatever it took to get it for her.

Suddenly the pinto sniffed loudly. Winona immediately leaned forward to cover its muzzle so it would not nicker if it had caught the scent of another horse.

Hundreds of yards off, something materialized among the trees.

It took Winona a while to make out the outline of a horse and rider, so skillfully did the man blend into the background. He was scouring the brush, seeking her, no doubt. As she watched, another rider appeared. This one was not so skillful. It was a man in a wide-brimmed hat such as she had seen Mexicans wear down in Apache country.

Winona knew of a half-dozen Mexicans who called

the mountains their home. All made their living as trappers or traders. This man, her intuition told her, most definitely did not.

The pair sat there for the longest while searching for her. Then the skilled one melted into the vegetation and the Mexican followed suit.

Winona was in no hurry to come out of hiding. Where there were two, there might be more. She planned on staying there until she was sure they were long gone, then she would fly to the village and warn the Shoshones there were enemies in the area. Her uncle Spotted Bull, her cousin Touch The Clouds, and prominent men like Drags The Rope and White Wolf would rouse the warriors of her tribe to hunt down the invaders and either drive them off or slay them to the last man.

Time dragged by. Winona decided that she had waited long enough. She was reaching for the reins when to her rear a twig snapped.

Shifting, Winona felt her blood run cold at the sight of a vague form on horseback moving slowly toward her. They had known where she was all along! They were closing in!

With a slap of her muscular legs, Winona urged the mare into a gallop. Racing around the thicket, she headed to the northwest, making a beeline for the village.

The next moment two more riders popped up in front of her, barring her path.

Winona slanted to the left and took a slope on the fly. She bent low to better distribute her weight. At the top she twisted and was perturbed to see four men were now after her. One was the Mexican. Two others were white. The last had the swarthy complexion of a breed.

At breakneck speed Winona went down the opposite slope. She wound among dense pines and presently came on a stand of aspens. Into these she plunged, moving into the heart of the stand where the thin trees were pressed so tightly together that the mare had difficulty squeezing through.

There was a method to her apparent madness. Winona counted on her pursuers following her in. Their bigger mounts would have more trouble than the mare getting through. It should slow them down enough for her to make her getaway.

But when Winona emerged on the far side and checked to see if her ruse had worked, she saw the riders separate. Two bore to the left, two to the right. They were too smart for her. They were going around the aspens.

A flick of the reins goaded the pinto onward. Winona held the rifle in her left hand. Her long hair streamed in her wake. A meadow unfolded ahead, so she let the mare have its head. When she was close to the next tract of trees, she looked over a shoulder.

The four men were still after her. In the lead was one of the whites, a grizzled, grinning lodgepole of a man who wore a round hat made of black bear fur.

Winona had half a mind to shoot him. Since she might need every shot she had if they overtook her, she raced on. The mare flowed smoothly over the ground and betrayed no sign of tiring.

It soon became clear, though, that the man in the bear hat had a faster animal. Slowly but surely his sorrel gained. His grin widened. He had a rifle, slung over his back by means of a wide leather strap across his scrawny chest, but he did not try to unlimber it to shoot the mare out from under her. He did, however, take what appeared to be a coil of brown rope from off his left shoulder and held it in his right hand.

Black Powder

Winona worked her legs, urging the pinto to exert itself even more. The mare had a heart of gold, as her husband would say, and did its best, head low, legs flying. Onward through the forest they sped, hurtling logs, barreling through patches of brush.

To Winona's delight, she held her own. The man on the sorrel did not gain on her any more than he already had. The other men were much further behind, so far back that she did not even consider them much of a threat.

Then, without warning, the forest ended at the base of a steep slope. And not just any slope. It was covered by talus from top to bottom, by broken bits of rock of all sizes. Loose, slippery rocks that offered no firm footing for man or beast.

Winona had no choice. If she tried to go around, the man on the sorrel would be on her before she got halfway around the hill. She had to go up the talus slope and hope the mare kept its footing all the way to the crest.

With the thought came action. Winona urged her mare to gallop straight up, and for 15 or 20 feet they made steady headway. Then the rocks started sliding out from under the mare's driving hooves. The horse slipped, righted itself, and went on, but slower now, because if it tried to gallop it would lose its purchase and go sliding back down to the bottom.

A mocking cackle made Winona glance back. The scrawny man was laughing at the mare's efforts. He had started up after them, his sorrel picking its way with uncanny skill. He still held the brown rope, but close to his leg where she could not see it well.

Winona smiled grimly to herself. She would give the scrawny one something to cackle about when he got a little closer! Hunching forward to better distribute her weight, she poked the mare gently with the stock of her rifle. The pinto, muscles rippling, climbed steadily.

A dozen feet higher, and they came to where the talus consisted of mainly small, flat rocks as slippery as shale. The mare lost her footing, recovered, then promptly lost it again. With every step the animal took, the talus spewed on down the slope. It was next to impossible for the horse to plant all four legs firmly.

Winona patted its neck to encourage it. The animal was slick with sweat and had to be tired, but it gamely plodded higher. More and more rocks clattered out from under it.

The next moment the mare's rear legs buckled. The pinto dug in its hooves and tried to push upright, but as it did a whole section of talus under its front legs gave way.

The next thing Winona knew, the horse was on its belly and sliding downward at a fast clip. She hauled on the reins. The mare tried its utmost to stand but there was no footing at all. Its legs churned. It nickered. It toppled onto its side.

Winona had to scramble to keep from being pinned. She clung in helpless frustration to the side of her saddle, yet another gift from her adoring husband. There was nothing else she could do until they came to a stop.

Twenty feet lower, they finally did. Winona carefully stood and stepped back so the mare could rise unburdened. The short hairs at the nape of her neck prickled as that mocking cackle was repeated very close behind her. She whirled.

The scrawny man sat astride his sorrel not six feet away, gazing at her in frank amusement. "I'll say this for you, squaw, you gave us a hell of a chase. But now you're ours."

Black Powder

A cold fury seized Winona. She gave him a taste of his own medicine, mocking him with a laugh of her own, and said, "You have it all wrong, white dog. Now you are mine." With that, she brought up the Hawken.

Fleeting surprise registered on the grizzled man's face. Then his right arm flicked up and out. The brown rope flashed toward her. Only it wasn't a rope at all. Too late, she saw it was a whip such as she had seen white men use who drove big wagons pulled by many oxen or mules. A bullwhip, it was called. And this man was a master at using his.

The tip of the whip wrapped itself around the muzzle of the Hawken. Before Winona could prevent it, the rifle was torn from her grasp and jerked out of her reach. Undaunted, she grabbed for a pistol. Her right hand closed on the smooth wooden grip and she started to swing the flintlock up even as her thumb curled back the hammer.

The whip cracked a second time, its rawhide coils looping around Winona's ankles. Just as she aimed and squeezed the trigger, she was wrenched off her feet.

Winona's right elbow smashed onto the hard rocks. Involuntarily, her finger tightened on the trigger and the flintlock went off. She did not mean to shoot. It just happened. A strident whinny greeted the booming retort of the .55-caliber smoothbore. Lusty curses exploded from the scrawny man.

The coils around Winona's ankles slackened. Kicking and wriggling her legs, she cast them off her and pushed to her feet.

The sorrel was down. A large hole in the center of its forehead oozed blood and brains. Its tongue lolled out, and its body quivered as if it were cold.

Partially pinned under the dead animal was the

man with the whip. He struggled mightily but could not free himself. Glaring at Winona, he snarled, "You bitch! You killed Buck! The best damn horse I've ever owned, and you killed him!"

Winona reached for her other pistol. "Just as I am going to do to you."

The scrawny man recoiled. He extended a hand, palm out. "Now you hold on there, squaw! You don't want to be doing that! I wasn't tryin' to hurt you. Just capture you, is all."

"I am Shoshone. You are my enemy. There is nothing more to be said." Winona began to level the flintlock.

Then a rifle blasted at the bottom of the talus slope. A lead ball whined off nearby rocks. The other three men had arrived. Another was taking aim as Winona ducked down so that they could not see her over the dead horse.

The man in the bear hide hat continued to grunt and push against his saddle, to no avail. He muttered to himself, a string of oaths such as her husband would never use.

Winona saw the three men below dismount and climb. One was reloading. His companions had their rifles trained, ready to shoot her when she reappeared. Or would they? Winona wondered. The scrawny one had just told her that they wanted to take her alive. Maybe they would hold their fire long enough for her to escape.

Using the pinto was out of the question. The mare had kept on trying to rise and had slid another fifteen feet lower. With it had gone Winona's ammo pouch and powder horn, which she had placed in a parfleche tied to the back of the saddle. She had no way to reload. And her rifle lay well past the sorrel, out in the open.

The way Winona saw it, her only hope lay in reaching the summit and losing herself in the forest. It would take her pursuers time to pry their friend from under the horse and scale the slope. She regretted having to leave the mare and her effects behind, but it could not be helped.

Besides, Winona would get them back when she returned with dozens of warriors and tracked the quartet down.

Girding her legs, Winona wedged the spent pistol under her sash, waited until all three men were looking down at the loose rocks under their feet, and made her move. Springing up, but staying doubled at the waist, she sprinted toward the crest. She zigzagged to throw off their aim. And it was well she did, because a rifle cracked and lead ricocheted inches from her right leg.

The scrawny man let out with a bellow. "Hold your fire, Owens, you brainless bastard! Comanches don't pay for cripples!"

Comanches? Winona mused on the run. What did Comanches have to do with anything? She took five more bounding leaps and suddenly the answer burst on her like an exploding keg of black powder. It nearly threw her off stride.

The men were slavers!

Until that moment Winona had assumed they were common bandits, men who roamed the mountains preying on anyone and everyone. Nate and she had tangled with their ilk before. But now she knew the truth, and she was sorry that she had not shot the scrawny one when she had the chance.

In early childhood Shoshone girls were warned by their mothers to beware the dreaded slavers. Winona remembered her own mother telling her about the vile bands which swooped down out of nowhere and made off with screaming women and young girls. She had been five or six at the time, and the tales had terrified her as nothing else ever had.

But the slavers never struck once while Winona was growing up. By the time Winona had seen twelve winters, she had come to suspect that the stories were just that. They were meant to keep little girls in line, to keep them from straying too far from the village.

The winter before Winona met Nate, events had shown her otherwise. One day a group of warriors from another Shoshone band showed up in the village. They were painted for war and wanted the help of Winona's father and others in hunting a band of slavers who had made off with eight women and four girls.

One of those girls Winona had known, a distant cousin named Falling Star, a favorite of hers. One summer they had spent fourteen whole sleeps together, playing and laughing and having a grand visit.

Her father and the other men had been gone a long time. When they came back, they hung their heads, and their shoulders were bowed. She could still remember the shock on her mother's face.

The warriors returned with just one of the captives. They had tried to save them all but the slavers had put up a bitter fight. Five of the warriors had been killed. The slavers had escaped, taking the rest of the women and girls with them.

Falling Star had been the only one rescued. Winona had dashed over to her friend to embrace her and tell her how happy she was that Falling Star was safe and well. But she had stopped short, horrified by the blank look on her cousin's face, by the dead eyes staring back at her.

Her cousin had never been the same afterward. It was the talk of the tribe for quite some time. Falling Star lived another two winters, refusing to eat or drink or tend to herself. Her parents had done the best they could, but in the end she had wasted away to mere skin and bones, and perished.

Ever after that, whenever Winona heard the slavers being mentioned, her insides would knot into a ball and she would clench her fists in impotent rage. She hated them with a passion more intense than any emotion she had ever felt except for her love for Nate and her children. If it were up to her, every slaver alive would be rounded up and thrown alive into a den of rattlesnakes.

And now four of the vilest creatures who ever lived were after her.

Winona dispelled her memories with a toss of her head as she came to the top of the slope. The three men with rifles had reached the sorrel and were in the act of freeing the scrawny man with the bull-whip. She was tempted to use her last shot to bring one of them down but she ran on, saving the ball in case she needed it later on.

Spruce trees and brush closed around her. Winona went a short distance westward, then bore to the north. She made a point of sticking to rocky ground. In the hard soil she left virtually no tracks. When she had been running for quite some time, she halted and crouched.

No sounds of pursuit fell on her ears. Winona felt some of the tension drain from her limbs. The slavers would never find her now. In two days she would reach the village if she held to a brisk pace and traveled half the night.

Winona went on. She avoided dry twigs and limbs which might snag on her dress. Repeatedly, she

51

looked back. So focused was she on the woodland she had covered that it was a while before she woke up to the fact that the forest ahead of her was unnaturally quiet. There should have been birds chirping, squirrels chattering, chipmunks darting about here and there. But it was as if the wildlife had vanished.

Or been cowed into silence.

The thought brought Winona to an abrupt halt. Only three things that she knew of would cause all the animals to go completely quiet. One was a roving grizzly. Another was a cougar, or painter, as the whites called them. The third occasion was when humans clashed in noisy battle.

Winona had seen no sign of a bear or a big cat. And the talus slope was so far behind her that the two shots and the shouting should not have had any effect on the wildlife.

Why, then, were the woods as still as a burial ground?

The flintlock clasped in her left hand, Winona warily advanced. She went around a wide pine, passed a cluster of boulders, and entered a clearing. About to cross, she glanced down and beheld a single footprint lightly etched in the dirt.

Winona would be the first to admit that she was not a seasoned tracker. She did know a fresh track when she saw one, though, and the print in front of her was new. It had been made by a heavy man wearing moccasins unlike any she had ever seen.

Few white men knew that no two Indian tribes made their moccasins the same way. Designs varied widely. Soles were shaped differently. Stitching patterns were also unique.

The Pawnees, for instance, preferred moccasins that were wider in the middle, while the Arapahos liked their moccasins to have wider toes. The Crows sewed their footwear in the shape of a half-moon. The Shoshones made theirs straight.

Winona did not know what to make of the strange footprint. She went to step over it and go on when an odd creaking noise drew her gaze up and to the right. In the time it took her to register the fact that a warrior in a breechcloth had been perched on a low limb and had just sprung, he was on her. She did not see the war club he held until a fraction of an instant before it slammed into the side of her head.

Then the world faded to black.

Chapter Five

Nate King leaped to his feet and ran after the young Bostonian to keep the man from getting them both killed. By all rights he should have caught hold of Simon Ward in just a few seconds. But fate conspired against him, for on his second step his left foot became entangled in grass that Ward had bent down, and before he could help himself, he pitched onto his face. "Wait!" he called out quietly enough not to be heard in the slaver camp. But he might as well have been addressing the wind.

Simon Ward heard. He just had no intention of stopping. His wife was in jeopardy. That was all that mattered. He did not care how many cutthroats he was up against. He was going to save her if it was the last thing he ever did.

The flickering flames of the fire served as a beacon. Simon cocked his new Hawken as he ran and held it close to his chest so it would not become caught in the grass. He spotted Felicity in the grip of a huge slaver in a coonskin cap who held the tip of a knife to her throat. A red veil seemed to shroud his vision. His blood raged in his veins. He hardly heard the words the man growled.

"If I tell you to eat, you'll eat! Don't pick at your stinking food like a damn bird! We want you healthy, woman. Not half starved."

Simon was almost to the edge of the trampled area. Some of the slavers had heard him and swung toward the grass, but he paid them no heed. Bellowing at the top of his lungs, "Let go of her, you scum!", he hurtled into the open and raised the Hawken to shoot the man in the coonskin cap.

Simultaneously, a breed near the fire stroked the trigger of his own rifle.

Everything happened so fast after that, Simon could not keep track. He heard the boom of the gun at the very same moment he felt a stunning blow to the ribs that knocked all the breath from his lungs. As if he were a feather, he was lifted into the air and hurled back into the grass. He came down head first and was too stunned to do more than feebly lift an arm. Then an iron clamp closed on the scruff of his neck and he was hoisted aloft again. Dimly, he was aware of grass parting in front of his face. It was a shock to realize that he was being carried, and he guessed by whom.

"Let go of me!"

"Shut up!" Nate King hissed. "They're after us, you fool."

"I've got to save her!" Simon protested. "They were going to stab her!" He fought to break loose, flailing his arms and legs.

"Idiot!"

That was the last Simon heard. An anvil smashed

into his chin, snapping his head backward. He saw the stars cavort in a dazzling display of pinwheeling lights which lasted only a few seconds. Then something seemed to swallow him whole.

Nate had no choice but to knock the greenhorn out. The slavers were closing on them like a pack of wolves on stricken prey. So far, they had not seen him, only Ward, and he wanted to keep it that way. He had a ten-yard lead, but it taxed his muscles to run at full speed while lugging a grown man under one arm who weighed in excess of 160 pounds.

Risking a glance back, Nate could see eight or nine bobbing heads. They were spread out in an uneven line, some closer to him than others. The rest of the band had stayed behind to safeguard their captive, as he had predicted.

Cutting to the right, Nate bent as low as he could and still go on running, burdened as he was by Ward. It would have been easier on him if he used both hands to hold the unconscious hothead, but he was not about to let go of his rifle.

Abruptly, Nate stopped and squatted. He sucked in a breath and held it. Motionless, silent, he listened to the crash of bodies all around him. A slaver passed within a few yards to his rear. Another went by directly ahead, so close that Nate could have swung his rifle and clipped the man on the head. But he did not budge.

Nate's plan was to lose himself in the high grass. In order to succeed, he had to do the unexpected, the very last thing the slavers would ever expect. So, when the onrushing line had gone on by, he turned *toward* their camp. Picking his way like a stalking painter, it was not long before he glimpsed the camp fire again. Immediately he changed course to the east to circle the trampled tract. Prudently he kept his eyes on those who had stayed behind.

The man called Gregor paced back and forth and glared at everyone and everything. In each huge hand he held a cocked pistol.

Felicity Ward was being held by two of the slavers. Tears drenched her cheeks. Nate figured that she had tried to go to her husband's aid. A rivulet of blood trickled from the right corner of her mouth, but otherwise she appeared unharmed.

Three other slavers stood near their leader, rifles tucked to their shoulders.

When Nate was almost all the way around the camp, he halted and lowered Ward. Simon groaned softly, not loud enough to be overheard, thankfully. With the rifle at his waist, Nate crept closer. If he could, he would like to spirit the woman out of there, but to attempt it now, with the slavers up in arms, would be certain suicide. Her fool of a husband had spoiled whatever hope they had of freeing her anytime soon; the slavers were bound to be on their guard for days.

Shouts broke out to the north. The slavers realized that he had given them the slip, and they were spreading out further in an attempt to run him down.

Nate was not worried. No one could track him in the dark, and it would take an army of men to probe among every blade of grass within 100 yards of the camp. All he had to do was sit tight until they tired and gave up. Then he could slip off unnoticed.

The big question was what to do afterward. Nate felt sorry for the Wards and wanted to help them, but by the same token he did not like the thought of being away from his family for a long time. And it was bound to take days, if not weeks, to rescue Felicity.

David Thompson

Simon sure as blazes couldn't do the job by himself, Nate reflected. The Bostonian would be as helpless as a newborn if left on his own. Just as helpless as Nate had once been, before his uncle and his mentor taught him how to meet the wilderness on its own terms and live to tell of it.

Nate glanced at Simon's prone form. As much as being separated from his family upset him, he couldn't bring himself to go off and leave the Wards. Not when they had no one else to depend on. He would have to do as McNair had done for him and teach Simon enough to get by. And in the bargain he had to come up with a brainstorm to save Mrs. Ward.

Commotion in the camp brought Nate's pondering to an end. Several of the slavers had returned. One was the beefy breed who had been so protective of Gregor. Nate had a hunch it was the same breed who had helped whisk Felicity Ward right out from under her husband's nose.

"We have lost him," the stocky one announced.

"How the hell could that happen, Santiago? You're supposed to be one of the best. What would your pa say?"

Nate knew that it was common practice among some of the Indian tribes living along the border of Mexico for the men to take Spanish names. In fact, the breed did look to be half Mexican. As for the other half, Nate could have sworn there were traces of Apache in the man's face and build. But that could not be. No self-respecting Apache, even one who was not full-blooded, would stoop to ride with slavers.

"I think maybe so there another," Santiago declared in broken, thickly accented English. "He help first get away."

"Two men?" Gregor said. "I only saw the one." He jabbed a pistol at Felicity Ward. "It was her jackass of a husband. And he couldn't give a five-year-old brat the slip in broad daylight. You know that. We dogged him for half a day before we swiped his woman."

"There maybe so two," Santiago insisted. "I not get good look at this other. But him big. Him very fast. Not stupid like husband."

Gregor tucked one of his pistols under his belt and scratched his chin, his brow knit. "I've never known you or your pa to be wrong before. And it is kind of peculiar that a fool like Ward was able to track us all this way. Maybe he had some help."

More slavers had returned. A short white man picked up Simon Ward's rifle, which had fallen at the edge of the grass. The stock of the new Hawken had been shattered. "Hey, lookee here," the man said. "This is why Santiago's shot didn't drop that yak dead."

"Ward is one lucky bastard," Gregor commented. He glanced at the string of horses, then at his captive. "Listen up. I'm not taking chances. Where there are two men, there might be more. So we're pushing on right this minute. I want half of you to saddle the animals and load up the packs while the rest fan out into the grass and stand lookout. Move it."

Whatever else might be said about the slavers, they were a well-knit group who obeyed their leader with military precision.

Nate suddenly saw several head in his general direction. Quickly moving to Ward, he knelt and draped the Bostonian over his left shoulder. Holding his rifle in his right hand, he moved deeper into the grass.

It should have been easy for Nate to keep from being discovered. Had he been by himself, he could have slipped away with the slavers being none the wiser. But Simon Ward chose that very moment to lift his head and give out with a groan loud enough to be heard in Canada.

Reaching back, Nate put a hand over the green-horn's mouth to stifle another cry. He need not have bothered. The damage had already been done.

"This way!" a slaver shouted. "I just heard them over here!"

"I want their heads!" Gregor roared. "A bigger share to the man who brings them down!"

Nate fled to the southeast, keeping low as before. He had to let go of Ward and when he did, Simon groaned again and tried to slide off him. Halting, Nate slid Ward off his shoulder.

The younger man plopped onto his knees and swayed like one drunk. "What the hell did you do to me, King? My jaw feels broken!"

"You'll be dead if you don't shut up," Nate whispered, once more covering Ward's mouth. "They're after us again."

Simon didn't care. He knew that the trapper had slugged him and he was outraged. The way he saw it, King had prevented him from saving his wife. He was befuddled. He was in pain. So he acted automatically and cocked a fist to pay the mountain man back.

Nate had about run out of patience with the man. Every time he tried to help, Ward gave him a hard time. Rather than try to explain, he punched Simon in the pit of the stomach. Not hard, just enough to cause the man to double over. As Ward did, Nate leaned down and said urgently into his ear, "If you ever want to see Felicity alive again, you had better come to your senses. We have to move, and move fast."

The mention of his wife's name cleared Simon's

head. He was still mad, but he decided to suspend their dispute for the time being and try to stay alive, for her sake. Gulping in air, his gut in agony, he pushed away the arm King extended and snapped, "All right. But don't think I'll forget that twice you've laid a hand on me."

"Come on," Nate said, moving silently off. He winced when Ward stumbled erect and followed, making as much noise as a small herd of buffalo. "Quiet!" he warned.

Off to the left a harsh voice rent the night. "Over this way! I just heard them!"

Whirling, Nate gave Simon a shove to hurry him along just as a shadowy figure bounded through the grass with a Kentucky rifle elevated to fire. Nate had his Hawken leveled at his waist. In a twinkling he cocked it and fired. The rifle belched smoke and lead and the charging slaver keeled over, discharging the Kentucky into the ground as he fell.

All hell broke loose. Shouts erupted. The flash of the two rifles had given the slavers something to shoot at, and they did. Guns cracked in all different directions. Lead balls whizzed every which way.

Nate dropped flat a heartbeat before the gunfire broke out and hoped his greenhorn companion had the presence of mind to do the same. Lethal hornets buzzed overhead and cleaved the grass to his right and his left. In the lull that followed the first volley, he jumped to his feet, scooped up the dead man's Kentucky, and turned.

Simon Ward stood a few feet away. The man had not bothered to duck down. Yet by some miracle he had been spared. "What is the matter with you?" he demanded. "One second you're pushing me, the next you're on the ground. What's it to be? Are we running or fighting?"

"Running," Nate said and gave him another shove just for the hell of it. The crackle of grass alerted him to oncoming slavers who would be on them in less than thirty seconds unless they made themselves scarce.

Simon heard the crash of heavy bodies, too. He realized there were far too many for the frontiersman and him to battle, so for once he did exactly as the trapper wanted and ran as fast as his legs could carry him. He had always considered himself fleet of foot and was confident he could outdistance their pursuers. But he soon found that racing through the grass was much harder than walking through it. The long stems clutched at his legs, seeking to ensnare him. Ruts kept cropping up, nearly tripping him again and again. To compound the situation, he had no idea if he was going in the right direction. In a very short time he worried that he might be running in circles, so he looked back to ask the mountain man. Only King wasn't there.

It had become apparent to Nate in the first few moments of the chase that Ward would not be able to outrun the slavers. Already the killers were much too close. Something had to be done to slow them down, and he was the only one who could do it.

Stopping, Nate squatted, set down his Hawken, and grasped the Kentucky by the barrel. Presently a burly shape loomed in the darkness, streaking after Simon Ward. The man never suspected that Nate was there.

Swinging with all the power in his broad shoulders, Nate clubbed the slaver on the side of the head. The man dropped like a poled ox. Nate threw down the busted Kentucky and picked up the man's rifle instead. Cocking the piece, he spied another slaver and fixed a hasty bead. At his shot, the man screeched, threw up his arms, and toppled.

Another ragged volley blistered the prairie. Nate was on the move before it rang out, taking the extra rifle along to give to Ward. He had not gone far when a man yelled.

"Hank is down! He's bleeding bad!"

"Forget him!" That sounded like Gregor, and he was awfully close. "I want the son of a bitch who shot him! No one is to turn back until then!"

Nate peered through the grass, trying to find the leader. Dropping Gregor was bound to distract the others long enough for Simon and him to make their escape. But the wily giant did not show himself.

Hastening on, Nate soon suspected that Simon must have changed course. He straightened to his full height to see above the tops of the grass, but he could not spot Ward anywhere ahead of him. With a start, he guessed that Simon had gotten all turned around and even then might be heading straight into the arms of the slavers. Pivoting, Nate headed back to save the greenhorn from his own incompetence.

Unknown to the frontiersman, not a dozen feet away Simon Ward huddled low in the grass. He had glimpsed a large figure to his rear, taken it for a slaver, and gone to ground. Now, as he heard the man move off, he smiled at his cleverness. It proved that he wasn't as helpless as Nate King liked to think.

Simon waited until he was sure the man had gone beyond earshot, then he rose and went on. He moved slowly. His right elbow brushed an object at his waist and he almost laughed out loud when he realized he still had both pistols and his butcher knife. In all the excitement, he had forgotten about them.

It reassured Simon to fill each hand with a heavy flintlock. Now he could defend himself. Using one of the pistols to part the grass as he had seen King do earlier, he hiked for several minutes. No more shouts broke out behind him. Nor did he hear anyone moving nearby.

Simon chuckled to himself. The high and mighty Nate King would be shocked to learn that he had given the slavers the slip all by his lonesome. Maybe, at last, King would regard him with a smidgen of respect. Simon didn't know exactly why that should matter to him, but it did. He had never wanted to impress any man as much as he wanted to impress the frontiersman. Maybe it was because, deep down, he liked King, and it would be nice if King liked him, too.

The object of Simon Ward's train of thought was at that very moment crouched within spitting distance of several slavers. He had discarded the extra rifle and held a cocked pistol. The slavers were talking in hushed tones, but he heard every word clearly.

"Two men dead, Gregor. Don't get riled at me, but I think we should give it up and get the blazes out of here before we lose any more. It's a mighty long ride between here and Texas. What with all the hostiles hereabouts, we need every man we've got."

The slaver leader growled like an irate bear. "Damn that greenhorn and his partner all to hell! It galls me to let them get away. But you've got a point, Jenks."

"What about Hank, Pedor and Vin?" asked the third man. "Can we tote them back now?"

"Do it," Gregor said.

Nate lowered onto his stomach as more slavers joined the trio. Orders were issued. The two men he had shot and the one he had knocked out were carted off. Nate did not move until the tramp of feet dwindled. Then he rose and cat-footed in their wake, seeking Simon Ward.

Black Powder

It would be totally in keeping with the Bostonian's character for Simon to be working his way back to the slaver camp to make another attempt to free Felicity. Ward wouldn't care that he didn't have a snowball's chance in Hades of whisking her away by himself. He would get himself rubbed out and leave her worse off than she had been before.

Nate hoped to keep that from happening. Every few yards he would rise and risk being spotted so he could scan the prairie on all sides. If Ward was out there, for once the man was using his head and not showing himself.

In the distance the fire twinkled. The chase had covered close to 500 yards, more than Nate had figured. He dropped down when one of the slavers turned, the man's pale face like a tiny moon against the black backdrop of the plain.

Suddenly the grass to Nate's right quivered. Since all the slavers were in front of him, he thought it was Simon Ward and shifted with a smile of greeting on his face. Almost too late he saw the near naked figure of the half-breed and the dull glint of steel in the warrior's right hand.

Santiago was like greased lightning. He lunged and stabbed and would have buried his blade in the frontiersman's chest had Nate not been holding his rifle in front of him. As it was, in the dark Santiago misjudged the position of the barrel and his knife glanced off it.

Nate felt the blade tear into his shirt close to the ribs even as he threw himself backward. He tried to level the Hawken, but Santiago was on him before he could. The butcher knife cleaved the air. Nate had to let go of the rifle to grab the breed's stout wrist. The next moment they were on the ground, grappling, rolling back and forth as Santiago strained to thrust his blade into Nate and Nate strained to keep the knife at bay.

The breed was tremendously strong, one of the strongest men Nate had ever fought. Their faces were inches apart, and he could see the feral gleam of bloodlust in Santiago's dark eyes. Flipping to the right, he heaved, trying to keep the warrior off balance long enough for him to draw his own knife. As his hand closed on the hilt, the breed's hand closed on his wrist.

Locked together, they exerted their sinews to the utmost. Nate blocked a knee to the groin and countered with a head butt to the jaw, which rocked Santiago backward. But instead of weakening, Santiago roared like a berserk grizzly, opened his mouth wide, and swooped his gleaming teeth toward Nate's throat.

In the nick of time, Nate jerked his head to one side. The breed's teeth sheared into the fleshy part of his shoulder instead of the soft tissue in his neck. Excruciating anguish rippled down his body. Blood splattered his skin. Nate threw himself backward to break Santiago's grip and nearly cried out when his shoulder was torn open.

Santiago reared up, a patch of buckskin and a flap of skin hanging from his bloody lips. He spat them out, bent back his head, and howled like a demented coyote.

Nate drove his forehead into the breed's gut. It was like slamming into a wall. His blow had no effect on Santiago, but it did make Nate's senses spin.

Another second, and everything went from bad to worse.

Santiago wrenched his knife arm loose and arced it on high to deliver a final blow, while from the vicinity of the camp raced other slavers. One killer shouted "Hold on, Santiago! We're on our way!"

But the breed was not about to wait. Venting a howl of savage glee, he stabbed downward.

Chapter Six

It was night when Winona King revived. She didn't open her eyes right away, but she knew it was dark by the cool air and the brisk north-westerly breeze. That, and the small fire crackling a few feet away.

Winona listened to what was going on around her. Two men were talking in Spanish while a third hummed softly to himself. They had to be slavers, she deduced. But that meant the Indian who had taken her by surprise was one of the band.

As if to confirm her hunch, a low, clipped voice spoke in the tongue of her husband. "Woman awake, Ricket. She pretend not be."

"Is that a fact, Chipota?" answered the voice of the grizzled lodgepole in the bearskin hat. "Well, let's test her and see."

Winona heard someone chuckle. Since they

knew she had come around, she was about to open her eyes when searing agony lanced her left arm. Sitting bolt upright, she bit her lip to keep from crying out and glared at the source of her pain.

Ricket had taken a burning brand from the fire and pressed it against her wrist. Casting it down, he cackled and slapped his thigh. "You were right, Chipota, just like always. How in the world did you know?"

The Indian in the breechcloth squatted on the other side of the fire from Winona. In its glow she could note details she had missed earlier. He was an older warrior, in his fifties or early sixties, with wide grey streaks in his long hair. "Her breathing not same," he explained.

"Sharp ears you've got there," Ricket said. "Too bad your sprout ain't along. He'd be right proud of you."

Chipota shifted his cold gaze from the fire to the grizzled slaver. "Santiago not sprout," he said flatly.

Ricket laughed. "Don't get your dander up, Injun. It's not an insult to call someone a sprout. All I meant is that he's a heap younger than you. And you can't fault me there."

The warrior grunted.

Winona rubbed the charred circle of skin where the brand had burned her and surveyed the camp. Five horses, including her mare, were off to the right, tied in a string. Two other slavers were playing cards to her left, while the fifth man kept busy cleaning a pistol. She was surprised that they had not had the foresight to bind her. It was a mistake they would rue.

"So how are you feelin', squaw?" Ricket addressed her. "That wallop on the head rattle your brains any?"

"I am fine," Winona said, when in truth her temples throbbed and she felt a little queasy.

"Good. We don't want the merchandise damaged, if you get my drift. We've got special plans for a woman of your caliber. Yessiree."

"You are slavers," Winona bluntly declared.

The grizzled scourge of the mountains and plains snickered. "Nothin' gets past you, does it, squaw? Yes, we are. And you know what that means. So just behave yourself and we'll get along right fine. Act up, and you'll sure as hell regret it. I can guarantee."

Winona lifted her chin in defiance. "My name is Winona King, slaver. And it is you who will regret it when my husband learns of what you have done. Grizzly Killer will not rest until he has tracked you down and made you pay."

"Grizzly Killer, is it?" Ricket said. "I'll admit that's some handle. Maybe around these parts it puts the fear of the Almighty into those who might raise a hand against you, but it doesn't mean diddly to us, squaw."

"It will."

Ricket squinted at her and gnawed on his lower lip. "You speak the white tongue better than most whites I know. Which means this Grizzly Killer of yours has to be white himself. What's his Christian name, woman?"

"Nate King," Winona said. She was proud of the fact that tales of her man's exploits had spread far beyond the Rocky Mountains, just like those of men like Jim Bridger, Kit Carson and Shakespeare McNair. She half hoped the slavers had heard of him, too. It might dispose them toward letting her go rather than face Nate's wrath.

"Can't say as the name is familiar," Ricket said, dashing fleeting hope on the hard rocks of reality. "I'll take it he's a trapper. Company man or free?"

"Free."

"How long has he been livin' in the wild? A short while?"

"As many winters as you have fingers and thumbs."

"Damn."

A slaver sporting a belly the size of a cooking pot raised his head from the five cards in his hand. "What's with all the questions, Ricket? Who cares about her husband? It wouldn't matter if he was Andrew Jackson himself. She's ours now, and that's all that counts."

The older man shook his head in mild reproach. "Owens, I swear that you don't have the brains God gave a turnip. If you did, you'd have guessed that I was askin' questions to find out if her man is as tough as she claims. And it sounds like he is."

"Oh?"

"Do I have to spell it out for you? King has lived in the mountains, among the Indians, for over *ten years*. Think about that. There aren't many men who can make the same claim. Most die within a year or two up in the high country." Ricket paused to spit. "That makes this Nate King the real Mc-Coy, a livin', breathin' fire-in-his-innards mountain man. And they can be meaner than hell when they get riled."

Owens yawned to show how impressed he was.

"Poke fun at me all you want to," Ricket said, "But I know what I'm talkin' about. Remember what Hugh Glass done."

"Who?"

Ricket rolled his eyes skyward. "Lord, spare me from peckerwoods who think with their hind ends." He folded his arms. "Hugh Glass is a mountain man. One time he got himself mauled something terrible by a big old she-bear. He was so torn up, his partners left him for dead. They took his rifle, his knife, everything. And off they went."

"And people say we're rotten to the core," another slaver joked.

"Pay attention," Ricket snapped. "You see, Glass didn't die. He crawled for days until he came on a dead buffalo swarming with buzzards and coyotes. Using nothin' but a stick, he chased them off and ate the meat himself. That gave him the strength to keep on going. Hundreds of miles he traveled, until he caught up with the men who had done him wrong."

Owens laid down a card. "So what's the point, old man?"

"If you don't know, it's hopeless."

Suddenly Chipota rose. "I keep watch. This night. All nights. Grizzly Killer come, I kill." So saying, he wagged his war club a few times, then moved off into the trees without making a sound.

Winona wished now that she had not told them about Nate. The gray-haired warrior would prove a formidable adversary, even for him. Her worry must have shown, because Ricket grinned at her and nodded at the spot where the warrior had disappeared.

"Chipota is the best there is at what he does, squaw. I bet you've never seen his like before."

"He reminds me of the Apaches," Winona said.

Ricket blinked. "You've been down in their neck of the woods? That's mighty interestin'. And you're danged near right. Chipota is a Lipan. His people live in the west part of Texas, mostly. The way he tells it, a long time ago the Lipans broke off from the rest of the Apaches and took to livin' by themselves. Why, nobody rightly knows."

"A true Apache would never ride with the likes of you."

"In most cases, no. But old Chipota got himself tossed out of the tribe for killin' another Lipan. He had nowhere else to go." The slaver snickered. "Him and that breed son of his were wanderin' across the Staked Plain when we came on them. Our boss could have had us shoot them down like dogs, but Gregor is a savvy cuss. He offered to let them throw in with our outfit, and Chipota agreed."

The revelation surprised Winona. "You are not the leader of the slavers? Another is?"

The man called Owens and another one chuckled. "Do you really reckon we'd be dumb enough to have an old coot like him tell us what to do?" the former declared. "Hell, squaw. We wouldn't follow him to the outhouse."

Ricket frowned. "Pay him no mind, missy. Gregor, our boss, thinks right highly of me. That's why he put me in charge of this bunch here when we separated to go woman huntin'. Now that we've got you, we'll head for the rendezvous spot. Should take us about two days, maybe three, to get there."

The news that there were more slavers was disheartening, but Winona did not show it. She could only keep her fingers crossed, as Nate would say, that he did not come alone to find her. Her uncle and Touch The Clouds would probably join him, as might several of his close friends. There should be more than enough to deal with the slavers. Then she remembered what had happened to her cousin, and she had to suppress a surge of panic.

"The rules are simple, squaw," Ricket continued. "You do what we say when we say it. You don't sass us. You don't ever try to escape. Behave yourself, and we'll get along right fine. The choice is yours."

Winona had figured as much. They needed to understand one thing, though. "I have my own rules, as you call them. If any of you lay a hand on me, I will scratch your eyes out. If you try to hold me down, I will tear your face open with my teeth. And if you tie me and then have your way, the very first time I am freed, I will do all in my power to kill you."

"Feisty wench, ain't you?" Ricket quipped. "Well, don't fret yourself on that score, squaw. Gregor is the one who decides if we get to or not. He'd shoot any of us stupid enough to take a taste without his say-so. You're safe enough until we hook up with him."

Winona did not like the lustful smirk the scrawny man wore. It hinted that she was in for a rude lesson when they rendezvoued with the leader. But what she had told him applied to this Gregor as well. If they thought she was bluffing, they would learn the hard way that she was not.

It was despicable that any woman should ever be forced to give herself to a man she did not want to be with. Or to do it for money, as Nate said some white women did. It was the very worst of violations. It degraded women to their core. It made them out to be like dogs, to be abused as their masters saw fit.

Winona had only ever shared her body with one

man. Long ago she had decided that he was the only one for her. She would never share herself with anyone else. And if the slavers thought differently, she would show them that she would rather die than let them dishonor her.

Simon Ward did not move until he was certain none of the slavers were anywhere near him. Then he rose and stood on the tips of his toes, trying to catch sight of the mountain man. He had no luck.

When a few more minutes went by and still Nate King failed to appear, Simon worried that something terrible had happened. As hard as it was for Simon to believe, it was possible that one of the slavers had taken the trapper by surprise and slit his throat before he could cry out.

Simon no longer deluded himself about his chances of saving Felicity without the frontiersman's help. He had nearly gotten himself killed by rushing into the slaver camp the way he had done. As it was, he had a nasty pain in the ribs on his left side where something, perhaps a bullet, had creased him. He'd felt under his shirt, but there was no blood or furrow.

His sore jaw only compounded Simon's misery. He rubbed it while mulling what to do and finally opted to slink back toward the camp to see if he could find Nate King. Holding the pistol out in front of him, Simon slowly moved forward.

In a short while Simon thought he heard low voices. Halting, he tried to make sense of the words but they were too faint. A lot of rustling ensued, fading rapidly toward the camp. The slavers were heading back, apparently.

Encouraged, Simon went on. He had not gone far when a racket broke out about 50 feet to the east of his position. It sounded as if a bull buffalo were barreling across the prairie. On listening closely, he guessed that it had to be two men in a tussle. He heard their grunts, heard the thud of a fist striking home.

Daring to rise on his toes once more, Simon saw a black silhouette rear up out of the grass. He could not make out many details. That the man was immensely powerful was proven by the struggling figure he had hoisted overhead. For a few heartbeats the tableau was frozen, then the big man swept the figure downward and there was a crack so loud it resembled the retort of a pistol. But Simon knew the truth. It had been a human spine breaking.

A slew of shouts signified that the slavers had heard the ruckus and were on their way back. "There!" one yelled. "There he is! I want his hide!"

Simon dropped down, but not before seeing the big man sprint off to the southeast. He figured that it had to be Nate King, but there was nothing he could do to help the trapper out. A single shot would draw the slavers like flies to honey. It was better for him to lay low until the hubbub died down.

So that was exactly what Simon Ward did. More shots thundered. After one of them, a gruff voice cried, "I think I nailed him! Close in! We've got the bastard now!"

Despair gnawed at Simon's soul at the thought of losing the frontiersman. He was so strongly tempted to leap up and blaze away that he had to will himself to stay right where he was for the time being.

The hunt seemed to go on forever. Several times slavers passed close to where Simon lay on his stomach, but none came close enough to spot him. He was relieved when at length someone bellowed that the search was over and the slavers hurried toward their camp.

A lot of noise wafted on the breeze. The clink of a tin pot, the rasp of a knife blade on a whetstone, the whinny of horses and the barked orders of the slaver leader.

Simon was shocked. By the sound of things, the cutthroats were preparing to head on out. Felicity would be toted along whether she wanted to be or not. And it would take him quite some time to catch up since his bay was close to a mile away.

Desperate measures were called for. Simon stalked toward the trampled area. There might be some means of freeing her if he stayed alert and seized the moment.

The camp swarmed with activity. Most of the animals had either been saddled or had packs thrown on them. Some slavers were mounted. Others were busy tying on more supplies. A huge man who had to be the leader stood near Felicity, along with a portly man in buckskins and a Mexican in a *sombrero*.

Simon's heart ached at the sight of his wife. She hung her head low, despondent, her arms limp at her sides. No one was holding her, but she made no attempt to flee. It was as if all the life had been drained from her except for that needed to draw breath. Simon did not comprehend why until he drew closer.

The leader was talking. "—-pout all you want to, woman, it won't change a thing. Your husband is dead. The sooner you face that fact, the better. As for the big guy who was with him, that jasper took a ball and has crawled off somewhere to die."

Simon was devastated on two counts. First, the vile slaver lied through his teeth about Simon being killed. The only reason Simon could think of for the slaver to do it was to break Felicity's spirit so she would go along meekly with whatever the man wanted.

Second, the news that Nate King had been shot shook him to his core. He needed the mountain man more than ever.

Then the notion came over Simon that maybe the bearish leader was lying about Nate, too. The frontiersman was as tough as twopenny nails. More than likely he had given the band the slip. Or so Simon prayed.

Soon the remaining horses were saddled and the remaining packs were tied on. One of the slavers extinguished the fire while the rest filed out of the camp, bearing due south.

Simon had blundered. In his eagerness to see Felicity, he had snuck within a few steps of the end of the grass. Now, with the riders passing by within a dozen paces of his hiding place, he stood in peril of being seen.

Hunkering, Simon tensed, awaiting the outcry that would bring the band swooping down on him like buzzards to a fresh kill. It was that very moment that the fire went out, blanketing him in welcome darkness. Unless the wind shifted, he just might avoid being noticed.

The slavers rode off in single file, some in pairs. In the forefront trotted the huge leader. In his left hand was the lead rope to the gelding Felicity had been thrown onto. Her ankles had been lashed together under the animal's belly to keep her from jumping down and running off.

It tore Simon in half to have to squat there

while the love of his life was led away by men every bit as vicious as the grizzlies he had heard so much about. Tears formed in the corners of his eyes as he waged an inner tug of war with his emotions. Part of him wanted to break down and blubber as he invariably did in times of stress. The other part of him wanted to be strong, to demonstrate the gumption that a grown man should have.

Gradually the creak of leather and the clop of hooves faded. Simon forlornly stood and sighed. "Felicity," he said softly. "My darling."

The only answer was the whisper of wind and the rustle of grass.

Simon let down the hammer on the pistol and shoved it under his belt. He was about to go look for Nate King when he spied a trio of black forms in the middle of the trampled circle.

Slavers! Simon's mind screamed. They had tricked him and left three men behind to fill him with lead when he showed himself. But they were not going to get him without a fight! Drawing both pistols, Simon burst into the open and took aim at the closest form. He was scared witless, but he was determined to resist. Felicity would know that he had gone down fighting on her behalf, which might lessen the sting of his failure to protect her.

The Bostonian had his fingers on the triggers and was beginning to squeeze when something about the three forms struck him as being extremely peculiar.

They were on their backs, one right next to the other. Not one had moved, even when he dashed out of the grass.

Holding his fire, Simon edged nearer. Inky puddles that were spreading under two of the men explained why they were so lifeless. He stopped next to the first and lowered his pistols.

One was white, another Mexican, the third either an Indian or a half-breed.

The white man had been shot in the sternum. The ball had cored his chest and exited high on the right shoulder, leaving a hole the size of Simon's fist.

The Mexican had also been shot, but in the face. The bullet had entered low on the left cheek, passed completely through the skull, and blown out a ragged cavity above the right ear. Of the two men, this one bled the most, bits and pieces of brain mixed with his blood.

Strangely enough, the Indian's body bore no evidence of a bullet or knife wound. Simon did note that the man's arms were bent at an unnatural angle, as if each were busted at the shoulders. It took him a few moments to conclude that it wasn't the arms, but the *spine* that had been broken, and he remembered the fight he had observed. This, then, was the man Nate King had snapped over a knee as other men might snap broomsticks.

But where was King now?

Fueled by that burning question, Simon hastened back into the sea of grass. It upset him that the trapper had not appeared after the slavers departed, and he began to dread that the leader had not been lying, that the slavers really had shot the mountain man.

Simon cupped a hand to his mouth and called out softly, "Mr. King? Nate? Where are you?"

To the west a wolf wailed its lonesome lament and received the same reply Simon did: silence.

He nervously tapped his foot, unable to decide whether he should search for the trapper or go retrieve their horses. It troubled him, the animals being left unguarded. Nighttime, he had been told, was when most big predators, like bears and cats, were abroad.

Suddenly, as if to show how right he was, a rumbling growl pierced the plain. It was much too close for comfort. Simon's breath quickened. He could not tell where the sound came from, so he turned in a complete circle, trying to spy the source. If a hungry grizzly had caught his scent, he was as good as dead. The old-timers in St. Louis had stressed that trying to drop a griz using a pistol was an exercise in futility unless the bear was close enough to touch. Of course, if one of the mighty behemoths was that close, it would be on a man before he could get off a shot.

A loud crunch brought goosebumps to Simon's flesh. Something was coming toward him. He saw its bulky shape, saw stems bending to its great weight. Overcome by terror, he back-pedaled and tried to aim the flintlocks. To his dismay, his hands shook so badly that he could not hold the barrels steady.

In another moment the shape lurched into full view. Indescribable relief flooded through Simon as he recognized Nate King. But his joy was short-lived, for the mountain man uttered a groan and fell with a thud at his very feet.

Chapter Seven

Felicity Ward had never know true sorrow until now.

Her life had been enough of an ordeal making the arduous trek west to satisfy her husband's craving for adventure. It had turned into a nightmare when the pair of smelly, greasy slavers had pounced on her just as she was about to remove her underclothes. The nightmare had become a living hell as the pair hustled her southward, the man called Gregor cuffing her whenever she opened her mouth and cursing her in the most horrid language imaginable.

Still, Felicity had entertained hope. She knew her husband would not abandon her to her fate. She looked for him to show up sooner or later and save her from the loathsome clutches of the despicable crew of perverts.

Then Felicity's fondest desire had come true.

Simon had appeared—only to be shot the instant he did. And now, according to her tormentors, her husband was dead, lying back on the prairie, riddled by bullets.

It was more than Felicity could endure.

For the first time since she was ten years old, Felicity cried. She had never been one of those women who wept over every little setback life had to offer, but this proved too much.

Despite her small size and seeming frailty, inwardly Felicity had strength few of her peers could match. It was this strength that had given her the courage to forsake all that she knew. It was this strength that had sustained her during the ungodly long journey from Boston to the Rockies. It was this strength she had relied on to see her through the many long years ahead of living high up in the remote recesses of the mountains, cut off from the civilization she so liked, deprived of the comfort of family and friends.

And why had Felicity been so willing to give up all that was safe and secure and familiar? For the same reason women had been making similar sacrifices since the dawn of time, for the love of her man.

Oh, Felicity knew that Simon was more bluster than he would ever admit. She knew that he let his imagination run rampant over his common sense. In short, she knew all his flaws, but she loved him anyway.

In that regard Felicity was like many of her sisters. Secretly, she had never considered herself truly attractive or witty or charming, or any of the other things Simon constantly told her she was. Secretly, she had doubted that she would ever marry, that any man would think her worthy of being a lifelong mate.

So when Simon Ward had shown an interest in her, Felicity had been surprised. When he had courted her, she had been amazed. And when he had proposed, she had been so grateful for his ardent love that his flaws paled in comparison.

Oh, Simon! Felicity mentally shrieked. Squeezing her eyes tight, she shut off the flow of tears. Reaching deep down into the heart of her being, she found her flickering strength and clung to it as a drowning person would cling to a floating log.

Then hooves pounded beside the gelding, and Felicity looked up to discover that Gregor had dropped back to ride next to her. She dabbed at her cheeks and held her head high.

The slaver chortled. "Still have some grit left, do you? Well, we'll rid you of that soon enough, woman. By the time we reach Texas, you'll lick my feet clean every morning and love doing it."

"Never!" Felicity declared, revolted.

"Think so?" Gregor's smile was that of a man supremely sure he was right. "Others have felt the same as you. More than I could count. And each and every one of them learned the error of their ways in time. That's the key to what I do. Time. I have all the time in the world to break you." His smile widened. "Even the wildest mustang will tame down eventually."

Felicity refused to be cowed. "I pray that you rot in Hell, you devil. If anyone has ever deserved eternal punishment, it's you."

The huge man found that amusing also. "Don't tell me. I've got another Christian on my hands. Tell me, Christian, where's this almighty God of yours? Why doesn't lightning crash down out of the sky and fry me for daring to lay a finger on you?" Gregor leaned toward her. "I'll tell you why, bitch. It's because there is no God. I'm proof of that."

"You flatter yourself," Felicity said, and was rocked by a slap to the face that left her cheek burning as if from a hundred bee stings.

"I warned you before. Don't insult me or you'll regret it." Gregor clucked to his mount and pulled ahead.

Felicity Ward watched him, her fists clenched so hard that her knuckles were white. There was the one to blame for her plight. There was the brute responsible for the death of the man she loved. And he was the one she was going to kill. The others would probably tear her to pieces afterward. But so what? She would gladly give her life to avenge her husband.

All Felicity needed was for any of the slavers to lower their guard for the few moments it would take her to grab a pistol or a knife.

Then Gregor would learn the truth the hard way. There was a Hell. And he was going to burn in it forever.

At that moment, many miles to the northwest, another woman was about to defy another band of slavers.

Winona King was not about to meekly do as Ricket wanted. His threats were wasted on her. She had fought Apaches, Blackfeet and grizzlies. She had survived flash floods, fire and drought. All of which had molded her into someone able to hold her own against anyone, anywhere.

So no sooner did three of the four slavers fall

asleep than Winona cracked her eyelids and awaited her chance. She had turned in hours ago, pretending to be asleep all that time. With the Lipan off in the forest, no one had been the wiser.

The Lipan. He was the one Winona had to keep her eyes skinned for, the one who could ruin her escape. She had no way of knowing where he was. He might be off in the trees, he might be so close that she could throw a pebble and hit him. Regardless, she had to try to get away now, before she was taken even farther from Shoshone territory.

Owens was the slaver standing guard. Or, rather, sitting guard, because once the others had commenced snoring he had plunked himself on a log and pulled his deck of cards from a shirt pocket. He had his back to the fire, and to her.

Winona glanced at each of the others in turn. Ricket had his mouth wide enough to snare low-flying birds. His snore was a throaty rumble worthy of a bear. It drowned out the snoring of the remaining pair, one of whom had covered his head with the top of his blanket.

Slowly, Winona tucked her legs to her chest, eased onto her hands and knees, and pushed to her feet. None of the sleepers reacted. Owens went on playing his card game. Solitaire. Nate had taught her how to play, but she had never been fond of it—not like she was of checkers or her very favorite, chess.

Winona needed a weapon. The slavers had gone to bed fully armed, with their rifles at their sides. Trying to slide one out from under a blanket would be too risky.

Stacked near the fire was enough wood to last the night. Among the broken limbs lay a short, thick piece, which would do nicely.

Never taking her eyes off Owens, Winona stooped and carefully lifted a few branches aside to get at the one she wanted. She quietly set each down to her left. Once, she froze as Owens leaned back and stretched. His head started to twist, and for a few awful moments, it appeared that he would turn and see her. But he was only relieving a kink in his neck.

The slaver bent over his cards again. Winona picked up the limb she wanted. Her hand barely fit around it. Sliding both hands to one end, she moved toward the log.

Again Owens glanced up. Again Winona stopped. He gazed at the same point in the forest, as if he had heard or sensed something there. Could it be the Lipan? Winona wondered. If so, the warrior was bound to thwart her escape attempt. But she had to see it through. She owed it to her loved ones. She owed it to herself.

Another long stride put Winona directly behind Owens. He had picked up the deck and was shuffling his cards. Winona raised her club as high as it would go, tensed every muscle in her body, and brought the branch down on the crown of Owens's head.

The thud of the blow landing was so loud that Winona was certain the others would hear. But they slumbered blissfully on as Owens oozed to the ground and lay with his hands and feet twitching.

Winona lost no time. Placing the branch down, she snatched a pistol from under the slaver's belt and was about to do the same with his butcher knife when her intuition blared. She looked into the trees at the same spot Owens had, and her blood chilled.

Rushing toward the camp was a stocky figure. His features were dappled by darkness, but Winona did not have to see them to know who it was.

Four long strides brought Winona to the pines along the north edge of the clearing. As the night closed around her, a series of piercing yips roused the slavers. Their jumbled voices rose into enraged bellows, and the noisiest of them all was Ricket. His next words were as clear as could be.

"After her, Chipota! Fetch her back, you hear! I want that bitch!"

Winona was going as fast as she could. She regretted that the Lipan had showed up before she could reach the horses and untie the mare. It would take her a week or more to reach the Shoshone village on foot, provided that she eluded the slavers.

The darkness worked in Winona's favor. It not only hid her, it hid her footprints. The Lipan would not be able to track her. But that did not mean that escaping would be easy. The warrior's senses were bound to be as sharp as a cougar's. Giving him the slip would tax her skill to the utmost.

Suddenly halting, Winona crouched and listened. To her rear rose the patter of moccasins, a patter that died just seconds after she stopped. She held her breath, knowing that the Lipan was no more than thirty feet away and waiting for her to make a sound, any sound.

Back in the clearing, Ricket was cursing a blue streak. He called Owens every foul name Winona had ever heard white men use, and many she did not know besides. His tantrum was to her benefit. So long as he kept ranting and raving, the Lipan would not be able to hear much. Certainly not the whisper of movement as she lowered herself to the ground and snaked through the under-growth.

Ricket didn't seem to know when to shut up. Winona smiled at the man's stupidity. She cov-ered a score of yards, then rose and continued on foot, confident that for the moment she had given the warrior the slip. After traveling another twenty yards, she broke into a run.

Soon the swearing faded away. All Winona heard now were typical night sounds; the rustling of trees by the wind, the cries of animals, both hunters and hunted, and the rasp of her own breath in her lungs. She came to a hill and bore to the right rather than slow herself down by go-ing up and over.

Winona settled into a steady rhythm. Her sole hope lay in putting a lot of distance behind her before dawn. Once the sun rose, the Lipan would be on her trail like a wolf on the scent of a flee-ing doe. She hoped that she would stumble on a stream long before then. Not even an Apache could track someone through running water.

As time went by and there was no evidence of pursuit, Winona felt the tension drain from her body. She also felt fingers of fatigue pluck at her mind. The blow to her head was having lingering effects. Every now and then a woozy sensation made her want to stop and rest, but she refused to give in to weakness. Not when her life hung in the balance.

All went well until Winona crossed a meadow and entered another belt of pines. Above her a roosting bird let out with raucous cries of alarm, evidently mistaking her for a predator. It was a jay, and it quieted down a minute later. But the harm had been done.

At high altitude sound carried much farther than down on the lowlands. This was true in the foothills as well, especially at night when the air was crisp and the wind usually stronger.

Winona knew that the Lipan had heard. He would suspect the cause and he would come investigate. She had to get out of there, and quickly.

Although she was winded, Winona steeled her legs and sprinted for hundreds of feet. Obstacles were hard to perceive in the dark, and she nearly collided with a log. Another time a low limb nearly ripped her face. When she could sprint no longer, she slowed to a walk.

Every so often Winona stopped and cocked her head. No alien sounds fell on her ears, but she knew better than to think the Lipan would make any. Apaches were like ghosts when they wanted to be. Their stamina, their speed, their stealth exceeded that of her own people. Which was understandable given that Apaches lived for war. For untold generations their creed had been to kill without being killed, to steal without being caught.

It was an hour or so after fleeing the clearing that Winona finally had to rest. The dizziness had returned, and with it a bout of nausea. She shuffled to a flat boulder and sank down, her arms between her legs, facing her back trail.

Nothing moved out there.

Yet.

As would any woman devoted to her family,

Winona turned her thoughts to her husband and her precious children. She missed them terribly and wished she was with them at that moment, snug and warm in their tepee.

Winona knew of other Shoshone women who had taken white men as mates, only to have their husbands go off and leave them once the men tired of trapping. Some of those women had given their husbands children. Seeing them always filled her heart with a secret dread that one day Nate would do the same to her, although deep down she knew that he never would.

Winona counted herself fortunate that Grizzly Killer was the exception to the rule. He was a man of firm beliefs who held to his commitments as rigidly as iron. He loved her and Zach and Evelyn and would never abandon them, come what may.

It saddened her to think that she might never see any of them again. They were the joys of her eye, her reasons for living. Without them her life would be an empty shell. If it were not for—

Winona stiffened, annoyed that she had let her attention wander when she had to stay fully alert. She anxiously scanned the forest, without result. Taking a breath, she shoved upright and went on.

Soon Winona came to a wide ravine. She stared in frustration at the opposite rim 25 feet away. There was no choice but to go around. Turning to the west, she stayed close to the edge so that when she reached the end, she would know it right away.

A sprawling thicket barred Winona's path. Rather than work her way around it, she elected to squeeze past on a narrow strip of bare earth bordering the steep drop. Wedging the pistol un-

David Thompson

der her sash to free both hands, she turned so that her back was to the ravine and sidled onto the strip.

By clasping the ends of thin limbs for balance, Winona briskly skirted over half the thicket. Suddenly the ground under her buckled. She felt it start to give and tried to throw herself to the right, but gravity would not be denied.

It was a horrible feeling, plummeting into the ravine in the dark with no idea of how far it was to the bottom or what lay below. Winona pictured her body being dashed to broken ruin on jagged boulders or impaled by a tree limb.

Then Winona hit. Her shoulders slammed onto barren ground and she found herself tumbling down an incline, going faster and faster. In vain she thrust out her hands to arrest her momentum, but all she accomplished was to tear skin from her palms and break several nails.

Her hip struck a small boulder. Winona nearly cried out. She did a cartwheel and crashed down onto her back. Dust spewed over her face, getting into her eyes and nose as she shot lower.

As abruptly as the fall had begun, it ended. Winona rammed into something hard, something big, and a black fog engulfed her. Vaguely, she heard pebbles and loose dirt raining down around her. For a while after that the night was still.

With a start, Winona came to. She was on her left side. Her left leg throbbed almost unbearably. Sitting up, she bit her lower lip to keep from crying out when the agony grew much worse. Fearing that she had broken a bone, she probed the leg and located a spot exquisitely tender to the lightest touch. She was bruised and gashed but nothing had busted.

Close by was another boulder. Propping herself against it, Winona painfully rose. She stared bleakly at the ravine walls. They were much too steep for her to climb. Unless there was another way out, she was trapped as effectively as if she had placed her foot into the serrated steel jaws of a bear trap.

But Winona refused to let despair sap her will. Fighting the torment, she limped westward. The floor of the ravine was littered with boulders and dead limbs, which had fallen from above. She rounded a slab of rock, stopping short at the sight of pale bones.

It was the skeleton of a deer, a buck. Winona figured that the animal had somehow blundered over the rim and fallen to its death. The only other possibility, that the buck had survived but had been unable to climb back out and had starved to death, was too unnerving to contemplate.

A bend loomed ahead. Winona paused to catch her breath. She idly gazed upward—and her heart skipped a beat. Framed against the backdrop of stars was the outline of a stocky human figure.

It had to be the Lipan.

Winona clawed at her waist for the pistol, only to learn it was not there. It had undoubtedly slipped loose when she fell. Now she was defenseless as well as boxed in. Her plight was next to hopeless, but still she would not admit defeat. Where there was life, there was hope.

The figure disappeared. Winona hurried on as best she was able, eager to find a way out of the ravine before the Lipan found a way down. She hustled around the bend and couldn't believe her eyes.

To the left the ravine wall ran another dozen yards but to the right the ravine ended, blending seamlessly into the forest. A tangle of brush and trees offered haven from the warrior. Pivoting on a heel, she made off to the north, passing several trees. At the next one she stopped to look back.

At that exact moment the Lipan emerged from the vegetation flanking the other side of the ravine. Apparently he thought that she was still in there, because he flattened against the wall and stalked in after her.

Winona dared not linger. The warrior would realize his mistake all too soon. She noticed a long limb lying next to the trunk. It made an ideal crutch.

Half running, half hopping, Winona fled. Her battered body protested every step. Her left leg would have buckled several times if not for the limb. She broke out in a cold sweat. Sheer willpower kept her going long after others would have collapsed.

Winona was so intent on simply moving her legs that she was taken unawares when the trees thinned and a bluff barred her path. Veering to the right, she hobbled along until she came to level ground once again.

It was best to push on, but Winona needed to rest a few moments. Just a few. She leaned on the limb and worked her left leg to keep it from cramping. Suddenly, without having heard a sound, she knew that she had run out of time. She knew that she was no longer alone. Straightening, she turned.

Black Powder

He stood ten feet away, the war club at his side, studying her intently as if she were a mystery he was trying to make sense of. There was no anger on his face, just curiosity. "You like jaguar. You quiet. You fast."

Winona did not know what to say. Compliments were the last thing she had expected.

"You make good Lipan." Chipota gestured. "Come now. Go back. Ricket want."

"You will not take me without a fight," Winona declared, planting her feet and holding the limb in front of her as if it were a lance. It made a pitiful weapon but it was all she had. "I will not go back."

Chipota sighed. "I not want hurt you. Savvy? Come. I not touch."

"It makes no difference. I do what I must."

The Lipan was on her before Winona could lift the limb to strike. Almost casually he swatted it aside, shifted, and drove the handle of his war club into her midsection. She doubled over and gasped for breath. The limb was torn from her grasp. Fingers as hard as stone locked in her hair, and her head was jerked upward.

"You brave woman. But you much foolish."

In response, Winona tried to claw his eyes. The Lipan pulled backward. One of her nails raked his left cheek, drawing blood. She coiled for another try, but he was not about to let her. The war club caught her on the tip of the jaw this time. Her legs would no longer support her weight, and the last sight she saw as she toppled was Chipota giving her that strange look of his. Then the hard earth rushed up to meet her face.

Chapter Eight

A sharp snap brought Simon Ward out of a fitful sleep. He had dozed off seated next to the fire, his arms crossed on his knees, his forehead resting on his right wrist.

Fearing that the slavers had returned, Simon leaped to his feet and swung from side to side, seeking a target to shoot. There were none. Another snap drew his gaze to the glowing crackling embers beside him, all that remained of the roaring flames he had going at one point. He grinned in relief. There was no cause to fret. The slavers were long gone.

And so was Felicity.

That thought erased the grin. Simon sadly lowered his arms and stepped over to where Nate King lay. It had taken every ounce of strength Simon possessed to drag the mountain man out of the grass. Rekindling the camp fire had not taken long since the slavers had left a mound of buffalo chips behind.

To keep wild beasts at bay, Simon had built the fire as large as he dared without setting the prairie itself on fire. Then he had sat down and tried to stay awake until dawn, a hopeless task given his near total exhaustion.

The Bostonian had done all he could for the frontiersman, which was not much. Nate King had suffered a shallow stab wound on his left side and a gunshot wound to the head, a furrow dug into his scalp above the right ear. Neither were life threatening.

Simon couldn't wait for the mountain man to come around so they could go after his wife. He nudged King's shoulder. When that brought no result, he shook Nate none too gently. All the trapper did was groan.

"Nate," Simon said loudly. "Rise and shine. Every minute we waste, Felicity gets further away."

The words echoed in Nate King's head as they might inside a cave. He struggled up out of a black pit, surprised and glad to be alive. The last thing he remembered was a volley fired by the slavers and an explosion inside his skull. "Simon?" he croaked. "Is that you?"

"It sure is," Simon said, laughing out of sheer joy. "You had me worried last night, friend. The slavers claimed that they'd killed you. I was scared to death I was on my own."

Nate blinked a few times and felt a chill ripple down his spine.

"Now we can go get the horses and head out after those butchers. If we push, we can catch them before nightfall, don't you think?"

"I'm afraid it won't be that simple."

"Why not?" Simon wanted to know. He was not going to stand for any more delays. This was the day

David Thompson

he would rescue his wife or perish in the attempt.

"I can't see."

"What?" Simon said, not sure he had heard correctly.

Nate swiveled his head to confirm it. All he saw was a gritty gray veil. "I can't see a thing. The shot I took to the head has done something to my eyes."

"No!" Simon exclaimed, more out of concern for his wife than for the man who had befriended him. To his credit, he realized he was not being considerate and placed a hand on the other man's broad shoulder. "What can I do? We don't have any water or food, but I'll go rustle up what I can if you want."

Propping both hands under him, Nate sat up. He ran his fingers along the furrow and winced. It was tender but not very deep, and it had not bled much. Bears had done more damage on occasion. Why, then, couldn't he see?

Nate recollected hearing of men stricken with head wounds who lost their powers of sight and speech. One man he'd heard tell of had reverted to being a small child and had to be waited on hand and foot or he would have died. Something similar must have happened to him. The big question was: How long would the effect last? Was it permanent, or would his eyesight return to normal sooner or later?

"Does this mean we can't go after my wife?" Simon inquired.

Every syllable was laced with raw anxiety. Nate could not blame the man. If it were his wife, he would feel the same. Closing his eyes, he pressed his fingers over the lids and rubbed lightly. It produced no change. The gray veil seemed there to stay.

Simon Ward felt the old urge to cry come over him. This new setback, coming on the heels of so many in a row, was almost more than he could bear. He resisted the urge, but only with supreme effort.

Nate did not waste time bewailing his fate. It had happened; he must make the best of it. To that end, he held out his hand and said, "Help me up. We have to get to the horses."

"And what then?" Simon asked, afraid that the mountain man intended to head for the Shoshone village.

"What else? We save your wife."

"But *how*? With you blind, we don't stand a prayer. I can't shoot or fight like you can. If the slavers spot us, we'll both wind up dead."

Nate reached in the direction of the younger man's voice. His hand fell on Ward's arm. "Listen to me, pilgrim. You can't give up. I don't think those vermin have laid a finger on Felicity yet, but they will before too long. Do you want that to happen?"

"Of course not. How can you even ask?"

Nate tucked his legs under him. "Then we leave right away. You'll have to be my eyes for the time being, until my sight returns."

Simon shook his head. The idea was too preposterous for words. Yet he had to admit that everything the trapper said was true. They were the only hope of salvation his wife had. As he assisted the frontiersman to rise, he remarked, "But what if it never does? I can't spirit her away from them all by my lonesome."

"You might have to," Nate said. Although he would never let on, deep down he was more upset than Ward. There was indeed a very good chance that he would never see again, and it frightened him as few other things could. For how could he hope to survive in the wilderness without his sight? He would be unable to trap. He would be unable to hunt. His wife would have to provide for the family. And while he knew that she would never complain, he could not bring himself to impose so heavy a burden on her.

"Which direction do I go?" Simon asked. For the life of him, he could not recall if the horses were due north, to the northwest, or to the northeast.

"Northwest," Nate said, and felt the other man take his sleeve. "That won't be necessary," he stated, refusing to be treated as if he were completely helpless. "I'll follow the sound of your footsteps."

"Suit yourself."

And so they headed out, Simon tramping along in the lead, making enough noise to scare off every snake and insect within 50 yards. It was easy for Nate to keep up. But so preoccupied was he with the calamity his family faced that they hiked for minutes before he thought of something he should have thought of sooner.

"Wait a minute. Do you have my guns?"

"No," Simon replied. "You didn't have any on you. Just your knife."

"Did you look for them? Do you have a rifle?"

Simon shook his head, then realized his error and answered, "No on both counts. But don't hold it against me. I wasn't about to go off and leave you while you were lying there helpless. Who knows what might have come along? A bear, maybe, or a cougar." He thought a moment and added as an afterthought, "Or hostile Indians, perhaps. Maybe those Blackfeet you were telling me about."

Nate doubted that was the real reason. Ward had not left his side because Ward had been afraid to. It was as simple as that. But the Bostonian was right about one thing. Nate couldn't hold it against him.

All too vividly, Nate could recollect his own anxious feelings when he first ventured to the frontier in the company of his uncle. There had been a time when every little noise had made him jump, when every shadow had been a concealed enemy. It had passed, as all things must. For a while, though, he had been just like Simon Ward.

"It couldn't be helped," Nate said. "After we fetch the horses, we'll go look for my rifle and any others we can find."

"But it will delay us even longer," Simon protested.

"We need guns," Nate insisted. "Unless you'd rather chuck rocks at the slavers if they catch us trying to free your wife."

In silence they hiked for close to ten minutes. Simon was annoyed, but he had to admit that the mountain man had a valid point. Knives and pistols were no match for Hawkens and Kentucky rifles.

So much time had gone by since they left the horses ground-hitched that Simon was dead certain the black stallion and his bay would be long gone. He figured the pair had drifted elsewhere while grazing and were now either halfway to Missouri or up in the high country somewhere. Which made him all the more surprised when he set eyes on them a few hundred feet away. They had strayed apart but were in the general vicinity of where they had been left.

"Well, I'll be damned," Simon declared, and told King what he saw.

"Horses usually won't go far when ground-hitched," Nate explained. "They keep stepping on the reins, and that stops them every time."

Simon chuckled to himself. On the trip west he had always picketed the animals securely using iron picket pins he had purchased in St. Louis. It never had occurred to him to just let the reins drag the ground.

Nate stepped forward, stuck two fingers into his

mouth, and whistled as shrilly as a marmot. The black stallion raised its head, flicked its tail, and nickered. Focusing on the sound, Nate slowly moved toward it.

The bay was not quite as glad to see Simon. It watched him approach, and when he was almost close enough to snag the reins, it snorted and shied, backing away from his hand. "Hold on, you," Simon said gruffly, which only made it retreat farther. Angry, he dashed forward and clamped hold of the reins. "Enough of this nonsense," he declared.

The bay had other ideas. Suddenly rearing, it tore the reins loose and went to flee. It only managed a few strides when a front leg stomped on the trailing reins, which brought the horse up short just as the trapper had claimed.

Changing his tactics, Simon smiled and spoke soothingly. "There, there fella. It's just me, you idiot. The man who owns you. The one who rode you for hundreds and hundreds of miles, day in and day out for weeks. It seems to me that you ought to know who I am."

The bay bobbed its head but did not attempt to run off a second time. Simon slowly took hold of the reins, then spent a while patting the animal's neck and scratching it behind the ears as he often did so it would calm down. That did the trick. Simon was able to climb on without another incident. As he forked leather, he was mildly disconcerted to see King already on the stallion and waiting for him a short way off.

"Sorry," Simon apologized. "This horse has the brains of a jackass."

"That makes him special," Nate responded. "Jackasses are smart animals. A few trappers I know own them, and they swear that jackasses can go longer without water and food than horses, and they're more sure-footed on narrow trails."

"Oh," Simon said. Not wanting to appear totally ignorant, he threw in, "Well, horses can go faster." Then he slapped his legs and trotted off. Once again he failed to keep in mind that the mountain man had been blinded, and when he realized his mistake and twisted to call out to King to follow him, he found the trapper only a few dozen feet behind the bay, riding along as if he did not have a worry in the world.

Simon didn't see how King did it. The man might have permanently lost his sight, yet he went on with his life as if nothing out of the ordinary had transpired. If it had happened to Simon, he knew that he would have blubbered like a baby and would be an utter emotional wreck for months to come, if not years.

It made Simon wish that he could take things in stride as calmly as the mountain man. He wondered how King did it, whether the man had always had a level disposition or whether the trapper had somehow learned to take what life had to offer without complaint.

Unknown to the Bostonian, his companion was plenty disturbed. Nate kept hoping that his vision would clear, and as more and more time went by and nothing happened he became more and more discouraged. He could not abide the thought of being a burden to Winona and his children. It would be better to die, he reckoned, than to inflict himself on them.

Or so Nate thought until he remembered old Otter Tail. Once a venerable warrior, Otter Tail had been wounded in a battle with raiding Bloods. An arrow had glanced off his skull. Afterward, he could no longer see.

Where others might have given in to sorrow and feelings of helplessness, Otter Tail had determined to carry on his life. He had worked hard and long to reacquire many of the skills he had before, and to improve on them. He became adept at making bows esteemed as the best in the tribe. He had his wife teach him to sew and he became an expert shield maker, as well. It was not long before warriors from many different bands were coming to him for their bows and shields. In his own way, he became a legend among the Shoshones, a shining example of what a person could do if they only put their mind to it.

Maybe, Nate mused, he should follow Otter Tail's example and make something of his life instead of throwing it away. But what could he do that others might benefit from? He certainly couldn't make bows. And his sewing was downright pathetic. He couldn't get the hang of using a sewing needle no matter how hard he tried. The last time he'd mended his own britches, he'd put more holes in his fingers and thumb than he had in the buckskin.

Nate was still mulling over his options when they reached the campsite. Simon reined up first and announced that they had arrived.

Swinging down, Nate said, "I'll stay here. It wouldn't do to have me clomping through the grass. I might ride right over a rifle and never know it."

Simon's first inclination was to insist that the trapper accompany him. Bears and buffalo roamed the high grass, and he didn't care to bump into either while alone. But as he watched Nate King grope the stallion's neck for the reins, he realized that the frontiersman would be of no help if a wild beast should appear.

"All right. I'll try not to take too long." Wheeling the bay, Simon rode into the grass, his hand on his pistol. He really thought that he was wasting his time. To his amazement, he had not gone ten yards when he came on Nate King's Hawken lying right out in the open. He knew it was the mountain man's because King had customized it with an inlaid silver plate engraved with his name.

Overjoyed, Simon went on. He was going to ride at random when it hit him that the search would be much more thorough if he adopted a regular pattern of working back and forth from east to west. Within five minutes he found another rifle and a pistol. The latter he nearly broke when the bay stepped on it. At the last moment he spotted the glint of metal and hauled back on the reins.

For quite some time after that, Simon's search was fruitless. When he looked up and saw that he had gone over 200 yards from the camp, he decided enough was enough and headed back. Partway there the polished stock of another pistol claimed his attention.

Beaming proudly, Simon rode back out into the open. Suddenly he stopped cold. Nate King was on one knee next to the three bodies, running a hand over the face of the dead Indian. It made Simon's flesh crawl. Sliding down, he walked on over.

"What are you doing?"

Nate slowly rose. "I was a mite curious. This coon nearly did me in." He absently placed a hand over the knife wound. "A few more inches to the left and I'd be worm food right now."

"How did you know the bodies were here?"

"I smelled them."

Simon took a long sniff and regretted it. There was a faint but distinctly foul odor he had not noticed before, which was bound to grow much worse before too long. "I'm surprised the coyotes and buzzards haven't treated themselves yet."

"The scent of the fire and all the slavers is still too strong," Nate said. "Once it fades, they'll feast." He raised his head. "Did you have any luck?"

"Did I!" Simon handed over the rifle and one of the pistols. He expected to be praised for a job well done, but all King said was "I'm obliged."

Not that Nate wasn't grateful, but he was more concerned over whether the Hawken had been damaged. He gingerly ran a hand over it, closely examining the stock, the barrel, the trigger and hammer.

Hawkens were next to impossible to come by on the frontier. Everyone Nate knew who owned one had bought it from the Hawken brothers in St. Louis, and there wasn't a trapper alive willing to part with his prize no matter how much he was offered.

Nate was glad to find his rifle intact. He set the stock on the ground, then uncapped his powder horn. Since he often measured how much black powder to use by pouring it into his palm until he had a pile a certain size, it was not that hard for him to do the same by touch alone. But funneling the powder into the barrel took some doing, as he simply couldn't upend his palm over the muzzle as he was wont to do. He had to cup his hand just so and let the grains trickle slowly.

Wedging the lead ball down on top of the powder proved to be no problem. All Nate had to do was take a ball from his ammo pouch, shove it partway in with his thumb, then slide the ramrod out of its housing, align it over the barrel, and push. When he had tapped the ball firmly into position, he replaced the ramrod.

"Not bad," Simon said, impressed.

"Practice makes perfect, even when you can't see what you're doing, I reckon," Nate replied. He reloaded the pistol, tucked it under his belt close to the buckle, and nodded. "I'm as ready as I'll ever be. Lead the way. You'll have to do the tracking."

Simon was about to turn. "Me?" he blurted. "You can't be serious."

"Never more so. The tracks will be as plain as day. There are eleven slavers left, plus your wife, plus extra horses." Nate mustered a wan grin. "They'll leave a trail a blind man could follow."

The frontiersman was proven right. Simon had not paid much attention to the tracks when he had hunted for the guns, but they were there and impossible to miss even though the slavers had ridden off in single file. The passage of so many horses had flattened a yard-wide path. Simon moved along at a trot.

Nate had no trouble keeping up. He was so used to riding the stallion that the two of them moved as one. Thankfully, there were no trees to dodge, no gullies to cross, just mile after mile of flat prairie.

The mountain man soon found that his other senses compensated to a degree for his eyes. He was able to gauge the passing of time by the warmth on his face. When it was warmest on his left cheek, Nate knew that the sun was to the east. When his forehead was warmest, the sun had reached its zenith. As the day waned, his right cheek warmed.

The breeze brought the strong smell of buffalo wallows to his nostrils. Nate also smelled the grass underfoot, the sweat on the stallion, and his own.

His ears told him exactly where Simon was, and enabled him to ride along without fear of colliding should the young man from Boston unexpectedly draw rein.

Toward evening the wind picked up, as it invariably did. Nate concentrated on the drum of the bay's hooves and sped up just enough to pull alongside it on the left. "We have to talk, Simon."

Ward had been thinking of all that had befallen him since his wife's abduction. On hindsight, he considered it a miracle that he was still alive. Barging into the slaver camp as he had done was without exception the most boneheaded stunt he'd ever pulled. He would not make the same mistake twice, he vowed.

While Simon's mother-in-law might be right about him having a head as dense as granite, he did know how to learn from his blunders.

On hearing his name, Simon glanced around. It took a few seconds for him to appreciate that the mountain man had actually called him by name this time, and not just 'greenhorn.' "About what, might I ask?"

"You have a decision to make."

"I do?"

"Your wife is the one in jeopardy. So you get to decide whether we push on through the night or make camp. I'll abide by whatever you choose to do."

Simon did not see where it was much of a decision. He couldn't abide the idea of Felicity spending another night in the clutches of the cutthroats. Who knew what they would do to her? But as he went to answer, he hesitated. King had been looking peaked the past few hours. Simon wondered if he should call a halt for the trapper's sake.

Before the Bostonian could speak up, however, a rumbling snort sounded just 18 feet away and an enormous shaggy bulk reared up out of the grass.

Black Powder

Simon Ward reined up and gaped in astonishment.

It was a bull buffalo. Worse, it was clearly annoyed at having its dust bath interrupted. And the next moment it lowered its massive head and pawed the ground, about to charge.

Chapter Nine

Felicity Ward did not get her chance that first day. She hoped and prayed that one of the slavers would be lax for the few seconds it would take her to snatch a pistol or knife. But they were skilled at their wicked craft and never let their guard down when close by.

It did not help matters any that the man called Gregor had evidently taken a fancy to her. The slaver leader kept her near him throughout the day. Repeatedly she found him ogling her on the sly. There was no misjudging his intent. It was the kind of look every woman knew all too well, the raw, bestial hungry look of a man in the fiery grip of lust. He wanted her. And knowing his temperament, it wouldn't be very long before he took what he wanted.

Felicity grew queasy just thinking about it. She would fight for her womanhood tooth and nail, but against a giant like Gregor the outcome was pre-ordained.

Black Powder

Toward evening the slavers called a halt. Since they had been on the go for almost 20 hours, men and animals were exhausted. They had stopped only twice, once at midday to give the animals a break and again in the middle of the afternoon when they came on a small stream.

Felicity would have given anything to be allowed to wash herself from head to toe, but she was not about to ask permission knowing that every man there would cluster around to whistle and make lewd comments. She had to tolerate being filthy, at least for a while yet.

Gregor had tossed her a blanket, told her to spread it out, and went off to arrange the camp to suit him. They were on the west bank of a narrow creek, in a clearing bordered by prairie grass and a few slender cottonwoods. Evidently the same site had been used by other travelers, because there were several charred remains of previous camp fires.

A burly slaver who was mostly Mexican but had blue eyes tended to their cooking. He was a wizard at mixing commonplace ingredients into savory meals. Throughout the day he had angled into the grass now and again, always returning with leaves or roots or tender shoots.

Now, with a stew thickened by chunks of rabbit meat boiling over the fire, Felicity sat on the blanket Gregor had spread out for her and pondered her next move. Since getting her hands on a gun or blade was out of the question, she had to make do with whatever else was handy. She scoured the ground for something, for *anything*, that would suffice as a weapon.

Gradually, the sun sank, blazing the western sky with bold strokes of red and orange. Despite it being summer, a number of distant peaks were crowned by ivory mantles of snow. It was so magnificent a scene that it moved Felicity in the depths of her soul, soothing her for the few moments she admired the heavenly spectacle.

The tramp of heavy feet brought her back to reality.

Felicity swiveled and could not help gulping at seeing Gregor leer at her as if she were a dainty morsel he was about to bite into. She held her chin high, crossed her legs, and folded her arms. Her anger flared when this provoked lecherous laughter.

"It won't do you no good to hide your charms, woman," Gregor said. "When I want them, they're mine. And there's not a damn thing you can do about it."

Locking her eyes on his, Felicity declared, "This I swear. I will kill you if you presume to lay a finger on me."

Again Gregor was merely amused. "I've heard that threat a hundred times if I've heard it once. And I'm still here. That ought to tell you something."

"It tells me that every rattlesnake has its day. But all things come to an end. Your time will come. I just pray to God that I'm there when it does."

Gregor's smirk changed to a scowl. "You have a mouth on you, woman. It will please me no end to tame you, to break you like I would a wild horse, to show you that the proper way for a woman to regard a man is as her master."

An unladylike snort burst from Felicity before she could stop herself. "You like to delude yourself, I see. But what else should I expect from a man who has to beat women into giving him what they would never offer on their own? You're worthless trash, Mr. Gregor. And nothing you say or do will ever make me change my opinion."

Felicity was looking right at him yet she never saw his leg move. The kick caught her high in the right

GET
4 FREE BOOKS!

You can have the best Westerns delivered to your door for less than what you'd pay in a bookstore or online. Sign up for one of our book clubs today, and we'll send you **4 FREE* BOOKS**, worth $23.96, just for trying it out...**with no obligation to buy, ever!**

————————◆•◆————————

Authors include classic writers such as
LOUIS L'AMOUR, MAX BRAND, ZANE GREY
and more; PLUS new authors such as
COTTON SMITH, TIM CHAMPLIN, JOHNNY D. BOGGS
and others.

————————◆•◆————————

As a book club member you also receive the following special benefits:
- **30% OFF** all orders through our website & telecenter!
- **Exclusive access to** special discounts!
- **Convenient** home delivery **and 10 days to return any books you don't want to keep.**

There is no minimum number of books to buy,
and you may cancel membership at any time.
See back to sign up!

*Please include $2.00 for shipping and handling.

YES! ☐

Sign me up for the Leisure Western Book Club and send my FOUR FREE BOOKS! If I choose to stay in the club, I will pay only $14.00* each month, a savings of $9.96!

NAME: _____

ADDRESS: _____

_____

TELEPHONE: _____

E-MAIL: _____

☐ **I WANT TO PAY BY CREDIT CARD.**

☐ VISA   ☐ MasterCard   ☐ DISCOVER

ACCOUNT #: _____

EXPIRATION DATE: _____

SIGNATURE: _____

Send this card along with $2.00 shipping & handling to:

**Leisure Western Book Club
20 Academy Street
Norwalk, CT 06850-4032**

Or fax (must include credit card information!) to: 610.995.9274.
You can also sign up online at www.dorchesterpub.com.

*Plus $2.00 for shipping. Offer open to residents of the U.S. and Canada only.
Canadian residents please call 1.800.481.9191 for pricing information.
If under 18, a parent or guardian must sign. Terms, prices and conditions subject to change. Subscription subject to acceptance. Dorchester Publishing reserves the right to reject any order or cancel any subscription.

JOIN NOW!

shoulder and knocked her onto her back. Stunned, she went to rise, but suddenly he was there, astride her, his knee gouging into her abdomen while his left hand wrenched her hair.

"Have a care, bitch!" the leader snarled. "You might fetch a pretty peso where we're going, but that won't stop me from gutting you like a fish if you keep mouthing off. I can always find another woman to sell to the Comanches or the Mexicans. Whether you want to or not, you will treat me with respect."

A sharp retort was on the tip of Felicity's tongue, but it was choked off by the slab of a fist ramming into her stomach. Agony such as she had never known racked her, making her gasp and squirm.

Gregor smiled. "That's what I like to see." He caressed her cheek, then tweaked it hard until she cried out. "Pain, woman. A person will do anything to be spared from pain. Before I'm done, you'll beg me to do the kind of things I'll warrant only your husband has ever done. And you'll love every minute." Sneering, he rose and walked off.

Felicity wanted to sit up, to be strong in front of the others, but her limbs were mush, her resolve weakened. She was helpless before his brute force and he knew it. Closing her eyes, she curled into a ball.

To the onlooking slavers, it appeared as if their captive had forsaken all hope and was in abject misery.

The truth was quite different. Felicity Ward was praying, as she had many times prayed as a small child when things were going badly. She prayed for a miracle, for someone or something to save her from the ordeal she faced.

In short, for a guardian angel.

Winona King was jarred into rejoining the world of the living by the motion of her mare as it scrambled down an embankment. Pounding waves of pain lanced her head and she almost cried out. It took a while for her sluggish mind to make sense of her bouncing stomach and her sore wrists and ankles.

The slavers had thrown her over the pinto, belly down, and lashed her hands to her legs.

Winona tried to unbend but couldn't. The circulation in her limbs had been cut off for so long that her arms and legs were practically numb. Her stomach felt as if it had been stomped on by a mule. And as if all that were not enough, she felt slightly sick. Not meaning to, she groaned.

"Well, well, well," said a familiar raspy voice. "Looks as if the squaw won't die, after all. She's a tough one, ain't she, Chipota?"

"Yes," the Lipan answered.

Winona could see neither of them. By craning her neck she saw a horse behind the mare and one in front of it, but she could not glimpse either rider. Suddenly another horse darted toward the mare, coming up beside her. She learned what it meant when Ricket barked an order.

"Don't you dare, Owens! You lay a finger on her and you'll answer to Gregor!"

"I owe her, damn it! You saw the knot she put on my noggin!" Owens challenged. "I should break every bone in her stinking body."

Winona flinched as the slaver's sorrel was ridden right into her. Not hard, but hard enough to set her head to renewed ringing and her shoulders to screaming in protest.

"You heard me!" Ricket stood his ground. "Harm her and Gregor will peel your hide! And I'll help hold you down for not listenin' to me."

Something jabbed Winona between the shoulder blades. She was sure it had been a rifle barrel. For a few harrowing moments she thought that Owens would disobey and shoot her. Then another horse whipped close to her and barreled the sorrel aside.

"That be enough," the Lipan declared. "No more hurt her."

Owens did not take kindly to having the warrior tell him what to do. "Who the hell do you think you are, Injun? I may have to listen to Gregor and to this old fart when Gregor puts him in charge, but I sure as hell don't have to stand for having a red son of a bitch like you—"

Whatever else Owens was going to say was cut short by the thud of a blow landing. Winona saw Owens crash onto his back beside the sorrel. He was livid. His rifle had slipped from his grasp, but he still had two pistols and he whisked a hand to one of them. He wasn't quite fast enough. Abruptly, he froze, his expression fearful.

"You draw," the Lipan said, "and I put knife in you."

Owens licked his lips, his eyes narrowing.

For a few seconds the issue hung in the balance, and then Ricket joined them. "I tell you," he grumbled, "havin' to deal with this bunch is like havin' a passel of younguns underfoot all the time. It's a pain in the backside." He paused. "Chipota, why don't you lower your arm? I know you can fling that pigsticker into a fly at ten paces, but Gregor would have a fit if you made wolf meat of this yack."

The warrior evidently complied, because Owens relaxed and took his hand off his flintlock. Plastering a smile on his face, he slowly sat up, saying, "I reckon I wasn't thinking straight, Chipota. I didn't mean what I called you. It's just that being conked on the head made me madder than hell. No hard feelings, eh?"

The Lipan grunted.

Winona had been ignored during the dispute. Now

she twisted to see Ricket regarding her with a wry grin. "What do you find so humorous?"

"Women. The whole bunch of you are more trouble than you're worth." Ricket shook his head. "Beats me what the Good Lord was thinkin' when he created females. Seems to me the world would have been a heap better off with just men." Clucking his horse forward, he took the mare's reins in hand and headed out.

Owens had risen. He glared at Winona as she went by, but he did not say anything, perhaps because the Lipan fell into step behind her.

Winona wondered why the warrior had come to her defense. She also pondered his behavior the night before, when he had acted reluctant to bring her back. Was it because they were both Indians? That seemed unlikely, since Apaches were notorious for regarding all other tribes as enemies. No, there had to be another reason, but Winona was at a loss to know what it might be.

By bending her body away from the pinto, Winona was able to note the position of the sun. She was surprised to learn it was late in the afternoon, which meant she had been unconscious all night and most of the day.

The ropes were biting deep into her flesh. Whoever had tied her had done the job much tighter than was necessary, leading Winona to suspect that Owens was to blame. It would be just like him to take petty revenge by making her suffer. She tried rubbing her wrists and ankles together to loosen her bonds, but it only made matters worse. The skin broke. Blood trickled down over her fingers.

Finally Winona glanced at Ricket. "I would be grateful if you untied me."

The slaver laughed without looking back. "Nope. I

don't think so. As soon as you got the chance, you'd head for the hills. I won't risk havin' you give us the slip a second time."

Winona was confronted by a dilemma. She could not continue to hang there. When they finally did stop, she would be unable to move until her circulation was restored. That might take hours. And during all that time she would be completely at the mercy of her captors. "What if I give you my word?"

This got Ricket's interest. He shifted in the saddle. "How's that, squaw-woman?"

"What if I give you my word that I will not try to escape? Will you untie me then?"

"And you expect me to believe you?" Ricket crackled. "You must think I'm awful stupid."

"I would not break my word," Winona insisted. And, in truth, she wouldn't. She was a woman of honor, just like her man. It was one of the things that had attracted her to him.

Many men, even Shoshone warriors, were not always honest in their dealings with their wives. They would fool around with other women, then lie if caught. They would stay out late gambling with buffalo-bone dice, then come back to the lodge and claim they had been at a council meeting.

But not her Nate. He never lied to her. And he would rather spend his evenings in her company than with rowdy friends who had nothing better to do with their time than tell tall tales and lose their hard-earned possessions at games of chance.

Honor. It was as important to both of them as life itself. When they said they would do something, they did it. When they made a vow, that vow was never broken. So when Winona gave her word, she sincerely meant to keep it.

But Ricket shook his head, his eyes twinkling.

"Maybe you're not lyin'. But I'm not the one to put you to the test. We'll leave that to Gregor. You'll just have to hang there until we rendezvous with him."

"And how long will that take?"

The slaver scratched his chin. "Oh, if we ride all night, we should be at Black Squirrel Creek shortly after sunrise tomorrow. That's where we're to meet up."

Winona knew that region of the prairie well. Black Squirrel Creek fed into the Arkansas River about a two-days' ride from Bent's Fort, where Nate and she had gone many times to trade and purchase supplies. She knew some of the men who lived at the fort, including William Bent himself, and Ceran St. Vrain, both good friends of Nate's. If only there were some way of getting word to them! They would arm every man at the fort and rally to her rescue.

Trying to keep any trace of excitement from her voice, Winona casually asked, "Will you be stopping at Bent's Fort before you head south?"

Ricket snickered. "If some of us do pay the fort a visit, you can be damn sure that you won't be taggin' along. Five or six men will stay behind to keep you company."

Winona slumped, dejected. She tried telling herself that all was not lost, that eventually she would regain her freedom. But the prospects were growing bleaker. Once Ricket's band rejoined the other slavers, the odds of her being able to give them the slip would be very slim.

At that very moment, to her surprise and the surprise of every other slaver, the Lipan unexpectedly goaded his horse up next to the mare, bent down, and with a flick of his long butcher knife, he slashed the rope binding her wrists.

"What the hell!" Owens cried.

Ricket reined up and wheeled his horse. "Hold on

there, Chipota. What in the world do you think you're doing?"

The Lipan did not respond. He moved his mount around to the other side of the mare and leaned over to cut the rope around Winona's ankles.

"Damn it all!" Ricket said. "Have you gone plumb loco on me?"

Winona needed to take advantage of the situation while it lasted. She reached up to grab the mare's mane. But the blood flow had been cut off for so long that her arm did not want to cooperate. It commenced tingling, then pulsed with pain. She arched her spine to raise her body high enough to hook her elbow over the pinto's neck and hung there a few moments, waiting for the agony to subside. Her other arm and both legs also started hurting.

Chipota had slid his knife into its sheath and now advanced to take the mare's reins from a stupefied Ricket. "I watch her now," he said.

The grizzled slaver looked as if he could not make up his mind whether to be outraged or to just let the warrior have his way. Ricket sputtered, then coughed, then glanced at the other slavers and back at the Lipan. "What in tarnation has gotten into you? I've never seen you act like this before."

"I watch her," Chipota said.

"We heard you the first time." Ricket pursed his lips and stared hard at Winona as if she were to blame. "If you want the responsibility, it's yours. But mark my words. Let her escape and you'll have to answer to Gregor. He won't like it if we lose a beauty like this one."

Chipota looked at Winona. For a fleeting instant she saw something in his eyes that she had not noticed before, something which explained everything and filled her with more dread than ever. In a very real sense she had gone from the frying pan into the fire, as her mate was fond of saying. The moment passed when Chipota turned his typical stony gaze on Owens.

"She not run off. She not be hurt. Savvy, white-eye?"

Owens bristled. "Why single me out, Injun? I'm not going to lay a finger on her. But I will laugh like hell when she slips a knife into you when you're not looking. You're a fool if you think that she won't." Lashing his reins, he turned and rode off.

Ricket speared a finger at Winona. "Do you see? Do you see all the trouble women make? You're all the same. Just like my fickle ma. She used to draw men to her like honey draws bears. I lost count of all the squabbles she caused. And you're no better." He moved off in a huff.

Winona wisely made no comment. She managed to swing her legs over the mare as Chipota resumed their trek. Now that she knew what was on his mind, she had to keep her eyes on him at all times. She would not put it past him to spirit her off so he could have her all to himself. Then she recalled that he had a son named Santiago riding with Gregor. Since it was unlikely Chipota would do anything to endanger his own flesh and blood, she should be safe until the two bands reunited.

Her arms and legs ached for hours. Winona rubbed both constantly to aid the circulation. Her scraped wrists stopped bleeding but bothered her whenever she moved them.

The sun headed for the western horizon. Winona was thirsty and hungry but too proud to ask for drink or food. Several times she caught Owens giving her a look such as someone might give an insect they intended to crush underfoot. She had made a bitter enemy who would stop at nothing to pay her back. Despite what Owens had told the Lipan, she dared not turn her back on him.

As the sun faded over the distant mountains, so did Winona's flickering hope begin to fade. With each passing moment she was being led farther from her loved ones. In a few days they would be well south of Bent's Fort, in country she did not know, where there were many enemies of the Shoshones, where every hand would be raised against her, as it were.

It was enough to discourage the bravest of souls.

As night descended, Winona King felt as if she were riding into the very heart of darkness. In more ways than one.

Felicity Ward lay on her back, a blanket hiked up under her chin, and trembled. She knew it would be soon now. Gregor would return and force himself on her. And she had nothing to fight him with except her teeth and her nails.

For the past several hours the slavers had been sipping whiskey, smoking pipes and playing cards. None were anywhere near her, but she knew better than to try to flee. They would catch her before she had gone 50 yards and punish her severely.

Felicity looked toward the fire and saw Gregor up-end a silver flask. She nearly jumped out of her skin when a hand touched her shoulder and someone whispered in her ear.

"Do not say a word, *senora*. Do not do anything to give me away. They can not see us here in the shadows, not when they are so close to the fire."

Bewildered, Felicity glanced around. Julio Trijillo was on his hands and knees beside her. She could not see his features. "What do you want?" she timidly asked.

"Take this. It is the best I can do."

Something long and hard was pressed into Felicity's hand. Before she could question him further, the Mexican slipped noiselessly away. Moments later she saw him circle around into the firelight and stroll over to the others.

Lifting her hand, Felicity discovered a double-edged dagger. She could not believe her eyes. It defied reason for one of the slavers to aid her. Yet Julio *was* the only one who had treated her kindly since her capture. He was not like the rest. Even Gregor had admitted as much. Why he should help her, she had no idea.

A footstep sounded close by. Frightened that Gregor was on his way over, Felicity shoved the dagger under the blanket and looked up. It was only one of the others going off into the high grass.

Felicity fingered the smooth hilt and steeled herself for what she had to do. Over an hour went by, an hour during which her every nerve was on edge. Then, at last, she saw the giant rise and shuffle toward her. She gripped the dagger and held it close to her bosom, ready to thrust when he lifted the blanket off her.

The man reeked of whiskey and sweat. Swaying slightly, he knelt on the edge of the blanket and leered at her. "The time has come, bitch," he said, slurring every word. His huge arm extended toward her. "You're about to learn that I mean what I say."

The dagger suddenly felt much heavier than it was. Felicity trembled. She feared that she would start shaking uncontrollably and not be able to carry through with what she had to do.

Just then, shots rang out.

Chapter Ten

Several hours earlier and not all that many miles to the north, Simon Ward stared in shock at the enormous shaggy brute of a buffalo blowing noisily through its flared nostrils and pawing the ground as if it were about to attack.

On the long journey west Simon had seen many buffalo, but always at a distance. The mountain men in St. Louis had warned him about the dangers of getting too close. Buffalo were as unpredictable as bears, they had told him. Where one might flee at the sight of a human, another might attack. It was best to fight shy of them at all times.

Simon had not needed encouragement to avoid the huge beasts. They sported wicked sets of hooked horns that could disembowel a man or another animal with a single toss of their massive heads. The average bull stood as high as his horse. The biggest ones weighed over a thousand pounds. They were more formidable than grizzlies—and much more numerous.

The mountaineers had told Simon tales of poor souls caught in stampedes, their bodies crushed to pulped bits of flesh and bone. He had heard of one trapper who unwittingly stumbled on a bull in a wallow; both man and mount had been torn to ribbons by the enraged buffalo.

Now, seeing one at such close range, all those stories filtered through Simon's mind, filling him with fear. He lifted the reins to flee. But as he did, he noticed Nate King. The trapper had reined up a few yards past him and was turning his head every which way to pinpoint the buffalo's exact location.

It occurred to Simon that if the bull were to charge, it would bowl over Nate first, giving him the time he needed to escape. All it would take to trigger the charge was for him to whirl and gallop off. But he couldn't bring himself to sacrifice the frontiersman just to save his skin. Not after all King had done for him. Not if he wanted to be able to look at his own reflection again without being sick to his stomach.

"Don't move, Nate," Simon whispered. "It's a bull, and it's looking right at us."

Nate could hear the thump-thump-thump of the animal's heavy hooves tearing into the soil. It gave him a fair idea of how close the monster was, of the peril they were in. "What about its head?" he whispered back.

"Its head?" Simon repeated, perplexed. "The head is on its shoulders, right where it should be."

"No. I meant, does the bull have its head up or down?" Nate asked urgently.

"Up." Simon didn't see what that had to do with anything. He sucked in a breath as the buffalo took a step toward them. If it came at them, he would shout to try and lure it away from the trapper.

"Keep your eyes on it," Nate said. "Buffalo lower their heads when they're making ready to charge. We'll have a second or two to act. Give a yell and I'll draw it off while you head for the hills."

Simon stared at the trapper in amazement, ignoring King's admonition. The man had been blinded and was virtually helpless. Yet he offered to divert the bull so Simon could get away! What manner of men were these mountaineers, as they liked to call themselves? he mused. Did they not know the meaning of fear?

Then the bull rumbled loudly deep in his barrel chest. Simon swung around and saw its head dip. "Look out!" he bellowed. "It's going to attack us!"

Nate King promptly let out a yip while cutting the black stallion to the left and raking its flanks with his heels. He bent low as the horse erupted into a gallop. It was a calculated move on his part to lure the bull after him and not after the Bostonian.

And while it might seem to be an act of rank madness, there was method to it.

The black stallion was far superior to Ward's city-bred bay. Nate had received it in trade from a Shoshone famous for the quality of his war stallions. This particular black was one of the fleetest in the entire Shoshone nation, with powers of endurance that far surpassed most others.

Of the two horses, the stallion had the better chance of eluding the buffalo.

Nate did not need to be told that his ploy had

worked, that the bull was bearing down on him and not Ward. It snorted like a steam engine, its powerful legs pumping like pistons. He whipped the reins and bent forward, flowing with the driving rhythm of the stallion, adjusting to it rather than making it adjust to him as inexperienced riders were prone to do. He could not see a thing, but he did not need to. The stallion saw for both of them.

Nate had the illusion of flying over the earth. The wind fanned his face, his hair, the whangs on his buckskins. He held the Hawken close to his left side so it would not slip loose.

Behind the trapper thundered death on four hooves. The bull was incredibly fast for its size and bulk. It had a lumbering, awkward gait, which was oddly fluid at the same time. Over short distances, it was as fast as any animal alive.

That was the key to Nate's survival. The stallion had to outlast the monster. For if the horse could maintain its lead over the first few hundred yards, the bull would tire and give up.

Simon Ward had also wheeled his mount as the buffalo surged toward them. He drew up, though, when he saw it veer after the trapper. "Try me!" he shouted without result. Thinking that he might be able to plant a ball in the creature if he could overtake it, he raced after them.

Nate had to rely on his ears to gauge the gap between the stallion and onrushing doom. He could tell that the bull slowly gained. The stallion was already galloping flat out; there was nothing he could do but await the outcome.

Suddenly Nate felt a change in the stallion's gait, just such a change as he often felt when he made it hurtle an obstacle. It had to mean there was something in front of them. But what? Another buffalo? A whole herd?

Nate almost succumbed to panic in that terrible moment of uncertainty. But he had faced worse moments before; the raging assault of a berserk grizzly, the frenzied onslaught of a hostile war party, the feral fury of a vicious painter. He composed himself and flattened close to the stallion's neck. Whatever it was, he must trust in the stallion to do what had to be done.

Anxious moments passed. Nate clamped his legs and thighs tight. The stallion launched into a series of rolling bounds, which culminated in a tremendous leap. Nate knew that whatever they were vaulting had to be big or wide or both. He tried not to think of what would happen should the stallion land off balance.

Then the big black alighted. It stumbled, whinnied, and righted itself.

Nate would have been unhorsed had he not been holding on for dear life. He heard a bellow and a crash behind him. The stallion raced on. Soon he realized that the bull was no longer after them so he slowed, puzzled.

Simon Ward knew why. He had glimpsed a wide dry wash moments before the stallion leaped. It had seemed to him to be an impossible jump. He was certain that the horse would miss the far rim, fall to the bottom, and be attacked by the bull before it could rise.

By some miracle, the stallion made it. Barely. Then the bull went over the edge in a headlong rush. It slipped and slid to the bottom in a spray of dust. There, it turned to the right instead of going up the steep side, and pounded eastward. The last Simon saw of it was as it disappeared around a sharp bend.

At a hail from Simon, Nate turned and headed back. It was only then that he noticed that the gray veil which he had been seeing since being shot had brightened to a white haze. And when he glanced down at the stallion, he thought he detected a vague hint of motion and substance where before there had been nothing at all.

"Be careful," Simon called out. "You're almost to the edge of that wash."

"So that's what it was," Nate responded. He let the stallion take it nice and slow to the bottom. The big black hesitated, then went up the opposite slope with its rear legs pumping.

"That was too close for comfort, if you ask me," Simon commented. "For a few seconds there, I thought that buffalo had you for sure."

Nate had already put the incident from his mind. It was just one of many such narrow escapes he'd had since taking up the life of a free trapper. He had reached the point where he took them in stride as a matter of course. They were normal, everyday affairs, hardly meriting a second thought.

"What did you decide about making camp?" Nate asked.

In all the excitement, Simon had forgotten about the question the mountain man had asked him earlier. "If it's all the same to you, I'd rather push on. I wouldn't be able to sleep much anyway."

"Then that's what we'll do," Nate said. "Once it's dark enough, you'll have to keep your eyes skinned to the south for the glow of a camp fire."

As before, Simon assumed the lead. He couldn't say why, but he had the feeling that their luck had changed, that it wouldn't be long before he set eyes on his wife again. And he made himself a promise. Once she was safe, he was going to let her decide whether they went on up into the mountains or headed back for civilization.

Ever since her abduction, Simon had been thinking about his decision to come live on the frontier. And the more he pondered, the more it seemed to him that he had been taking Felicity for granted. In his enthusiasm, he had failed to take her feelings into account.

Back in Boston he had gone on and on about the wonderful life they would forge for themselves in the wilderness without *once* asking her whether she wanted to or not. He had waxed eloquent about the freedom they would enjoy without giving the dangers due attention. It had never occurred to him that she might prefer to live where she did not have to worry about being set upon by a wild beast every time she went out the front door. Or that she might actually want to buy her food at a market rather than grow it in the wild. He'd just assumed that she'd want to do the same thing he wanted to do.

Well, no more, Simon reflected. In the future he would always ask her opinion and give her an equal voice in all their decisions. It was the least she deserved for giving him the greatest gift any man could ever receive: the love of a good woman.

Time passed. A myriad of stars sparkled overhead. The lingering heat of the day gave way to the brisk coolness of night. Coyotes and wolves were in full chorus, punctuated every now and then by the throaty coughs of grizzlies and the piercing caterwauling of cougars.

Simon glued his gaze to the south, vibrant with anticipation, longing to spy the firefly glimmer of the slavers' fire.

Nate King, meanwhile, kept craning his neck skyward and squinting. His longing was to detect a faint gleam of starlight against the backdrop of inky ether. But try as he might, he could not do it. Apparently his vision was going to take much longer to restore itself than he would like, if it ever did.

Much later, Simon Ward glanced to the west, toward the black sawtooth wall formed by the distant foothills and mountains. He began to stretch, idly turned to the east, and caught himself, mystified by what he saw. He reined up.

Nate heard and did the same. "What is it?" he inquired. "Why did you stop?"

"It's a camp fire," Simon reported.

"Then we've done it. We've caught up."

"But it's not to the south, as you figured it would be. It's southeast of us. I'm not much of a judge, but I'd say it's three or four miles off at the most."

Nate was picturing the lay of the land in his mind's eye. He roughly calculated how many miles they had gone that day, and announced, "Black Squirrel Creek. That's where they've stopped."

Simon lifted his reins. He couldn't wait to see Felicity again, to hold her in his arms, to apologize for placing her in jeopardy with his insane dream. "Let's go!" he exclaimed.

"Hold on," Nate said. He didn't want a repeat of their last attempt to save Mrs. Ward. "Didn't you learn anything at all last time?"

"Don't fret. I'm not about to go rushing in there and get us killed."

That was good for Nate to hear. He was about to detail his plan for saving the Bostonian's wife when the night was rent by the far off blast of gunfire. Before Nate could say or do anything, Simon Ward cried out, "My wife!", and took off like a bat out of hell toward the slaver camp.

There were two shots, followed by loud whoops. That was all. But since they came from the strip of grass near the horse string, it was enough to send the startled animals into a panic. Some reared. Some kicked and plunged in an effort to break loose.

The slavers forgot all else in their haste to safeguard their mounts. They rushed toward the animals with their rifles in hand. Someone shouted that they were under attack by Indians, and several of the cutthroats opened fire, adding to the uproar and confusion.

The slaver leader, Gregor, had spun on hearing the first shots. "What the hell!" he declared. Shaking his head to clear it, he raced toward the string, leaving Felicity Ward alone under the blanket.

She sat up, terrified of being pounced on by hostiles, and recoiled when a figure burst out of the grass toward her. She was all set to slash with the dagger. Then she saw that it was Julio Trijillo. "What—?" she blurted.

The Mexican never slowed. Grabbing her hand, he hauled her to her feet, saying, "There is no time to explain, senora. You must come with me, pronto."

Felicity was in a whirl. she did not know what was going on. But since Julio had befriended her, she figured that he intended to save her from the hostiles. Nodding, she meekly let him lead her off into the grass. As soon as the blades closed around them, he ducked low and motioned for her to do the same.

"What about the Indians?" Felicity asked while trying her utmost to stick to the swift pace the man had set.

"There are none. That was me."

A feather could have floored Felicity. "Why did you do such a thing?"

"Why else?" Julio paused to check behind them. "It was the only way I could get you away from them."

Felicity wanted to ask him a score of questions, but he motioned for her to be silent. Then he angled to the right, moving rapidly, parallel to the camp. Some of the horses had quieted, but the rest were still giving the slavers a hard time. She could hear their lusty curses. Over the din rose Gregor's roars.

"It will not be long before they notice we are gone," Julio said over a shoulder. "We must ride like the wind if we are to get you to safety."

Ride *what*? Felicity was about to inquire when a pair of horses materialized out of the gloom.

Trijillo boosted her onto a chestnut, swung onto a buttermilk, and made off at a canter. He kept his eyes on the camp and his hand on one of the fancy silver inlaid pistols he wore.

Unable to stifle her curiosity any longer, Felicity rode abreast of him and asked, "Why are you doing this? Why risk your life for someone you hardly know?" Deep down she dreaded that maybe, just maybe, the man had whisked her away from the slavers because he wanted her for himself. If so, he would find that she was going to be true to her husband at all costs. She still had the dagger, and she would use it if he forced her to.

"You are a lady, senora," Julio said. "I could not let them sell you to the Comanches, or worse." He looked at her. "I must tell you in case something happens to me. We never found your husband's body. There is a very good chance he is still alive."

Felicity's hopes soared. Could it be? Could it really be?

Black Powder

The Mexican rose in the stirrups for a few seconds to study the plain behind them. "As to why I do this, I am not one of those renegades, Senora Ward. Oh, I know what you are thinking. That I must be one because I rode with them. But I only joined to kill Gregor and as many of the others as I could take with me when the right time came along."

"Go on."

Trijillo faced northward. He spoke so softly that at times Felicity could barely understand him. "I had a sister, senora. Her name was Rosita. She was young and beautiful and had so much to look forward to. We lived on my father's *hacienda* near Samalayuca."

Felicity leaned to the left so she would not miss a word.

"One night Rosita turned in as she always did. The next morning the servants reported that she was missing. All the *vaqueros* on the *hacienda* joined in a great search. We found tracks leading to the northeast, toward the border, toward Comanche country."

"The slavers took your sister?" Felicity guessed, appalled.

"*Si*. Boundaries mean nothing to *bastardos* like these. They raid in your country, they raid in mine, and then they flee into the wilderness so they will not be caught." Julio bowed his head. "We lost their trail at the Rio Grande. Months went by and we gave up hope of ever seeing her again. Then we received word from a man who trades with the Comanches that she had been sold to a chief. She was one of his wives."

The yelling had died down behind them. Other than the drum of hooves, the night was still.

"My *padre*, he sent word to this chief. He offered to pay a large ransom in horses and guns if the Comanches would see that she was safely returned to us. The chief agreed." Julio passed a hand across his eyes. "The trader was to bring them to a certain spot in the hills where we were waiting. My sister became hysterical, saying that she never wanted to go back—"

"Whatever for?" Felicity interjected.

"Rosita was too ashamed. She did not want to have people staring at her the rest of her life, to have them pointing and whispering behind her back. She told the trader that she would not be able to bear the humiliation." The brother took a breath. "But the chief would have none of it. He wanted the ransom. So he threw her on a horse and made her go along."

Felicity hung on every word.

"Two days out from the Comanche village, they made camp for the night. Rosita had acted cheerful all day, as if she had accepted what was to happen." Julio swallowed. "But she only did so to trick them, so they would not suspect what she really had in mind."

"Oh, God."

"*Si.* She slit her wrists and bled to death." A bitter sound, half laugh, half snarl, issued from the man's throat. "The chief felt he still deserved the ransom, so he brought the body to us. We killed him and the seven warriors with him."

There was nothing more to be said, so Felicity merely listened.

"My parents were satisfied that justice had been served. But I was not. The Comanches were not the ones to blame for my sister's death. It was the slavers who should pay. So for two years I roamed over northern Mexico and parts of Texas trying to find the band responsible. I changed my name. I made friends with anyone and everyone suspected of dealing with slavers. In time I learned who had taken my sister, and I spread the word that I wanted to join them." Julio looked up. "Now here I am."

Profound sorrow welled up in Felicity. The man had spoiled his chance of getting revenge by saving her. "If you ask me, you were in the right place at the right time. If not for you, I'd soon share your sister's fate."

Julio did not say a thing for over a minute. "Perhaps you are right, senora. Perhaps it was meant for me to be with the slavers at just this time. Perhaps it was meant for me to balance the scales. They took an innocent life, and I save one." He glanced at her, the upper half of his face hidden by the black *sombrero*. "Just do me a favor, senora."

"Anything."

"Make it count for something. Make something special of your life. Do not be one of those who wastes the gift they are given."

Abruptly, to the south, the collective thunder of many hooves rolled across the benighted prairie.

"They are after us," Julio announced.

"But how did they know which way we went?" Felicity wondered. "They can't track us in the dark."

"They do not need to," the Mexican said. "Gregor is not stupid. He has never trusted me, that one. I think he has suspected all along and was just waiting for me to show my true colors." He rode faster and she kept pace. "Gregor knows that I will take you to your husband."

Onward they galloped, Felicity a few yards behind her savior. Repeatedly she glanced back, seeking some sign of their pursuers. Not that she was very worried. It was so dark that she believed it would be child's play to elude the slavers.

Then a horse and rider appeared as if out of no-

David Thompson

where. Only he was in front of them, not behind them. He pointed a pistol at Julio Trijillo and called out, "For what you did to my wife, you're going to die!"

Chapter Eleven

Winona King was not one to let circumstances dictate the course of her life. When they ran contrary to the best interests of her welfare and those of her family, she opposed them with every ounce of strength in her body. And when her physical prowess was not equal to the task, she relied on her wits.

Circumstances had forced Winona to try to persuade Ricket that she wouldn't escape. She had even offered to give her solemn word as proof of her certainty—and been turned down.

Chipota had then interfered and claimed possession of her. For the past few hours she had ridden along docilely enough, but she had no intention of doing so forever. She hadn't given her word to the Lipan. There was nothing keeping her there, except herself.

As the small band wound down out of the foothills with darkness all around them, Winona was con-

stantly on the alert for a means of gaining her freedom. She hoped that they'd pass close to extensive
thickets, or else possibly a dense tract of woodland.
Anywhere the brush would serve to slow the slavers
down while she made good her escape.

Ricket was too wily for her. He avoided exactly the
areas she looked for, as if he knew what was on her
mind and he was determined to foil her. When they
stopped briefly to rest their mounts, he made it a
point to hover nearby, his rifle in the crook of his left
elbow. She was not going to give them the slip if he
could help it.

If the Lipan observed Ricket's behavior, he did not
let on. He also did not appear to pay much attention
to Winona, although several times she felt his eyes
on her when he thought that she would not notice.

The hothead, Owens, gave Chipota a wide berth.
But he was not above glaring at Winona every
chance he got.

As for the others, they generally ignored her.

Which was just as well. Twice Winona had been
on the verge of making a break for it even though
the vegetation was too thin to screen her. In each
instance, just as she went to make her move, she realized that either Ricket or Owens or Chipota was
watching her on the sly.

Then they came to the top of a high ridge and
Winona saw the prairie just over the next hill. The
high grass offered her a ready haven if she could
reach it well ahead of the slavers.

To that end, Winona shifted slightly forward on
the mare without being obvious. Pretending to be
more tired than she was, she yawned and stretched.
As she lowered her arms, she placed both hands on
the pinto's neck.

Chipota stared straight ahead. Ricket was guiding

his animal down a short incline. Owens glanced her way, then went to follow Ricket.

This was the moment. There might not be another. Winona knew that they would punish her if they caught her, that she would be beaten, or worse, and trussed up whether the Lipan liked it or not.

The stakes justified the risk.

Whipping forward, Winona snatched the reins and yanked with all her might, tearing them out of the warrior's grasp even as she slapped her legs against the mare's sides and let out with a Shoshone war whoop.

The pinto took off as if its tail were on fire. Its first bound brought it alongside the Lipan. Chipota twisted and grabbed at her, but she was ready and ducked under his arms. Her left leg flicked out, catching the warrior in the side. The blow sent him flying. He tried to clutch the back of his horse as he fell, but his fingers found no purchase on its sweaty hide.

In a flash Winona bore down on Owens. He had already jerked around and brought his rifle up. By all rights he should have put a ball into her. But in the fraction of a second it took him to fix a hasty bead, Winona did the last thing he would ever expect her to do. She deliberately rode her mare right into his horse.

Shoulder against shoulder, the two animals collided. The mare was smaller but it had more momentum and was going downhill.

Owens cried out as his animal went over the edge of the incline. He let go of his rifle to seize his reins, but it was too late. His horse whinnied as it lost its footing and toppled.

Ricket was only six feet lower down. He yelled something, but the words were lost in the frantic squeals of the two horses as the hothead's mount rammed into his. Both slavers and their horses crashed to the ground, then slid toward the bottom in a jumbled heap.

It was just as Winona had planned. She came to the top of the incline but did not slow down. Leaning as far back as she could, she took the slope on the fly. She heard Owens curse as she whisked on by.

The mare came to a level stretch, and Winona cut to the right to a switchback, which would take her to the base of the ridge. A shot rang out above her. The slaver missed.

"Don't shoot, damn you!" Ricket yelled. "We want her alive!"

Winona had other ideas. The only way they would lay their hands on her again was if she were dead. Staying in the middle of the switchback where the footing was firmest, she swept around the first bend and made for the next lower down. She thought that she glimpsed a pinpoint of light off to the southeast. It was most likely a camp fire, but she was not about to slow down to confirm the fact.

One of the slavers was hard on her heels. Winona enjoyed a lead, but it was not big enough to suit her. She flicked the reins, urging the dependable mare to go even faster. It was a grave gamble on her part, since a single misstep would send them both tumbling down the ridge.

"Stop her!" Ricket was bellowing. "Damn it, somebody stop that squaw bitch!"

The switchback leveled off at the bottom, and Winona streaked around the low hill. Ahead rippled the sea of grass. She looked back and saw only one slaver. He was a beefy, bearded man whose buckskins were as greasy as the bottom of a cooking pot. Simpson was his name, and he had hardly spoken two words to her since her capture.

Winona smiled on reaching the edge of the prairie. The mare plunged in. The grass closed around them. Winona hugged the pinto so she would be harder to spot, but it did no good. The slaver had excellent eyesight. He didn't lose track of her.

It soon became apparent to Winona that she was not going to shake him. Simpson would chase her until his horse played out, or hers did.

The mare had superb stamina, but was it enough? Winona dared not fall into their clutches again. They would guard her every minute of every day until they sold her or did whatever else pleasured their vile minds. She would never have another chance to escape.

Desperate straits called for desperate measures. Once Winona took care of Simpson, she would be in the clear. How to go about it was the big question. An idea blossomed but she balked at carrying it out. It just might get her killed. Or, even worse, put her right back where she started.

Winona raced on. It quickly became evident that the mare was tiring sooner than she had counted on. She could hold off no longer. Either she put her plan into effect, or she might as well rein up and wait for Simpson. The thought hardened her features.

The wife of Grizzly Killer would never surrender her life or her dignity without doing all in her power to preserve both.

Hooking an arm over the pinto's neck and her foot over its back, Winona swung onto its right side. It was a feat Shoshone warriors often relied on in the heat of battle. So adept were some, that they could shoot a rifle or lose an arrow while at a full gallop.

Shoshone women, as a general rule, seldom practiced the trick. They had no reason to, since they rarely engaged in warfare from horseback. When enemies raided their villages, their duty was to protect their offspring and safeguard their lodges. Both were best done on foot.

When Shoshone warriors went on raids of their own, though, there were times when women went along. Mainly they were there to hold the horses while the men crept off into an enemy camp. Sometimes the raids would go all wrong. Their enemies would rally and chase after them. It was then that a woman had to be as good a rider as any man or suffer the fate of never seeing her people again.

Winona had gone on a few raids with her father and cousins when she was much younger. Beforehand, she had insisted that Touch The Clouds teach her the tricks of horsemanship at which he was so skilled. Consequently, she was one of the better women riders in her tribe.

She proved it now by traveling scores of yards while clinging to the side of the pounding mare as if she were a human fly. She counted on it being too dark for the slaver to notice that she had changed position.

The smooth tops of the grasses brushed her back, her legs. A constant loud swishing sounded in her ears.

Winona willed her tense muscles to relax. She needed her body limp or she might break a bone. A quick check showed Simpson well over 50 feet away. She stared eastward, waited a few more seconds, then pushed off from the mare.

The grass cushioned the brunt of the fall. Winona landed on her left shoulder and rolled a half-dozen feet. The instant she stopped, she rose up into a crouch and glided back to where she had landed.

Timing now became critical. Winona coiled her

legs, her every nerve stretched taut. The grass hid Simpson and his mount. She had to rely on her hearing alone to gauge his approach. Louder and louder grew the drumming of his animal's hooves. Suddenly it reared up out of the night just a few feet away to her left.

Winona was in motion the moment it appeared. A pair of lithe bounds brought her to the steed's side. Simpson was so intent on keeping track of the mare that he didn't realize she was there until her hands closed on his leg. She heaved upward.

The slaver uttered a startled squawk as he was sent flying. He attempted to grab hold of his saddle, but it all happened so fast that he was in midair before he knew it. His rifle went sailing. His horse kept on running.

Winona saw where he crashed down and bounded forward. She had but moments before he recovered and confronted her. Clasping her hands together, she balled them into a knot and raised her arms to strike the slaver before he could stand. Everything depended on her being able to knock him senseless quickly.

It wasn't meant to be.

A heavy foot speared out of the stems and caught Winona on the shins. The blow knocked her legs right out from under her. She came down on her hands and knees and immediately scrambled to her feet again.

Simpson stood, too, but much more slowly. A mocking grin curled his thick lips. He made no attempt to draw either of the pistols at his waist, nor the knife on his right hip. Brushing at a sleeve, he regarded her closely and said, "Damn, but you're a sly one. I never would have figured you to pull a trick like that in a million years."

David Thompson

Winona did not respond. Shoshone warriors believed it was the height of folly to talk while in the heat of battle. And she was in a battle for her very life, whether the slaver appreciated the fact or not.

"Well, you've had your fun," Simpson said. "Now we'll just wait here for my horse to come back. And it will, in a little bit. I trained it myself in case I was ever clipped by a tree limb or some such."

The man was too sure of himself for his own good. He stood there talking down to her when he should have been acting. Winona was close enough that all she had to do was lunge and fling her hands at his waist. She wanted either pistol. She got neither.

Simpson pivoted and slammed the flat of his right hand into her shoulder even as he whipped a leg in front of her.

Unable to stop in time, Winona was upended into the grass. Pain lanced her thigh as she hit the ground, but she suppressed it and leaped to her feet before the slaver could close in. To her surprise, Simpson merely stood there, smirking.

"You're a feisty squaw, ain't you? I admire that. I truly do. But you'd better behave yourself now. I don't cotton to red devils actin' up around their betters."

At last Winona understood. His scorn did not stem from the fact that she was a woman. No, it stemmed from his disdain for anyone who happened to be Indian. In a word, he was prejudiced, as were many of his kind who believed that the only good Indian was a dead Indian. He rated her as beneath contempt. He was about to learn differently.

Winona bowed her head as if he had her cowed. She let her shoulders droop and took a step backward.

"That's more like it," Simpson said, placing his

hands on his wide hips. "I knew you'd get it through your thick red head sooner or later that it wasn't worth your while to try anything." He started to glance over his shoulder. "Now where in tarnation is that blamed horse of mine?"

The slaver played right into Winona's hands. She launched herself at him, low down this time, and heard his fiery oath as her arms looped around his legs. Although Simpson was far too heavy for her to lift, she could and did get enough leverage to jerk his legs right out from under him. The man cursed again as he tottered and fell.

Winona rolled once to the right to avoid being pinned. Reversing herself, she snatched one of the flintlocks as Simpson struggled to stand. The barrel was not quite clear of the slaver's belt when he caught hold of the pistol and tried to wrest it from her grasp. For a few tense moments they struggled. There was a loud click. Winona looked down just as the flintlock went off.

It was only by accident that neither of them was struck. The ball smacked into the ground within a finger's width of the slaver's foot and made him madder than ever. Calling her every vile name Winona had ever heard white men use and some she had not, Simpson resorted to sheer brute force, tore the pistol from her grasp, and snapped it overhead to bash her in the head.

Winona could not possibly evade the blow. Trying to block it would only result in her being battered to her knees. So instead of doing either, she went on the offensive. She kicked Simpson in the right knee.

The roar of mixed torment and rage that the slaver vented would have done justice to a rampaging grizzly. Simpson staggered backward, sputtering and snarling. "You bitch! You filthy red bitch! You broke my damn knee!" He swung the pistol in a vicious backhand.

The swing was ill-timed and awkward. Winona skipped aside, closed in before he could regain his balance, and kicked him in the other knee. Simpson went down, tripping over his own feet and landing on his backside. His features screwed in agony, he hissed at her as might a furious serpent. Then he did something she did not expect. He flung the spent flintlock at her face.

Winona easily dodged it. The gesture seemed futile until she felt his calloused palms close on her ankles. He had hurled the pistol to distract her. His real intent had been to get his hands on her, to yank her down beside him as he now did.

"You're going to regret hurting me, squaw!" Simpson growled while in the act of throwing himself on top of her. His left hand held her right wrist in a vise. His legs pinned hers. His free hand touched her waist, then slid higher. "Guess how?"

Winona fought with a savagery born of desperation. She bucked. She kicked. She thrashed and pushed. But it was as if he weighed tons. All her effort, and she could hardly budge him. His hot, foul breath fanned her face. His sweaty skin was so close to hers that she could feel its warmth. He leered and raised his free hand to touch her breasts.

Never! Winona mentally shrieked.

Her plight seemed hopeless. Other women might have given up then and there and submitted to what they deemed inevitable. But Winona King refused to give in.

Long ago Nate had taught her a valuable lesson. It had been on a sunny summer afternoon when he was teaching her how to shoot a rifle. Their talk had gotten around to personal combat, and what she should do if she were ever beset by a stronger foe when no gun or knife was handy.

"Do whatever it takes," Nate had told her. "When your life is at stake, there are no rules. There's no right way and wrong way to defend yourself. Bite, scratch, claw, kick, do whatever it takes to come out on top."

Winona had grinned at the image of her biting someone.

"I'm serious," Nate insisted. "Anything goes. Tear a nose off, or an ear. Gouge an eye out. Do whatever it takes to preserve your life. Nothing else matters." He had taken her into his arms and gently kissed her. "Not where I'm concerned. Without you, my life would be empty."

Whatever it takes, her husband had said. Winona applied that philosophy now by bending her neck and sinking her teeth into the soft flesh on the left side of the slaver's neck. The ease with which her teeth sheared through the skin was amazing. Crinkly hairs got into her mouth. So did a bitter taste, then the salty tang of blood.

A feral howl was torn from Simpson's throat. In a reflex action he lunged backward, and in doing so caused more flesh to be torn wide. Her teeth lost their grip.

"Damn your bones!"

The slaver glared down at her, raw hatred seeming to crackle around him like a physical force. He let go of her wrist and streaked both hands to her throat.

"You're going to die, bitch! Do you hear me? I don't care what Gregor wants. You're mine!"

His spittle dripped onto Winona's cheek. She hardly noticed as she clawed impotently at his locked fingers. She did notice, however, the berserk gleam animating his features. In a very few moments he would make good on his threat unless she could think of a way to stop him. In vain she punched his face and neck.

Simpson was bleeding profusely but he didn't care. All that mattered to him was strangling the life from the captive who had brought him so much suffering. "Die, squaw! Die!" he cried, and squeezed even harder.

Felicity Ward was so shocked by the unexpected appearance of the rider that she did not think to rein up, as Julio Trijillo automatically did. It was just as well, because she rode directly between the pair just as her husband was about to fire. "Simon!" she exclaimed, and halted. Intense joy vied with amazed disbelief. "Don't shoot! He's a friend!"

Simon Ward came so close to accidentally shooting his beloved that forever after when he recalled this night, he would shudder and grow as cold as ice. His trigger finger was applying pressure when she filled his sights. For the life of him, he would never know how he managed to keep from firing. But he did, and with a jab of his heels he was beside her horse and holding her in his arms.

For a few precious seconds the husband and wife embraced, each overwhelmed by happiness so profound that their hearts felt near to bursting. There were so many things they wanted to say to one another. Fate did not give them the chance.

"Senora Ward," Julio said urgently. "We must ride on. Gregor and the rest will catch us if we do not."

Simon glanced at the Mexican. He wanted to learn who the man was, to discover why a slaver had befriended Felicity. But the rumble of approaching horses alerted him to the new danger they faced.

"Lead the way, friend," he said. "We'll be right behind you."

Now that Simon had been reunited with the woman who meant more to him than life itself, he was not going to let her out of his sight. Had speed not been essential, he would have insisted that she ride double with him just so he could relish the feel of her body being close to his and know that he wasn't dreaming, that they really and truly were together again.

Julio took the lead as requested. His *sombrero* slipped off his tousled hair and hung by a chin strap. He headed to the northeast instead of due north in the hope that it would throw the slavers off their scent.

Felicity galloped beside her husband. Again and again she glanced at him to reassure herself that he was actually there. Ever since Julio had told her that Simon might be alive, she had hoped against hope that he would find her. But she had been racked by troubling doubts. The prairie was vast, after all, and Simon was no Daniel Boone.

Yet there he was, grinning at her as he used to do when they were courting and they would go for long rides in the countryside surrounding Boston, his teeth a pale half-moon in the darkness.

Felicity smiled to show her own happiness, then knuckled down to the task of keeping up with Julio. He was going faster than ever, as if it were crucial that they put a lot of ground behind them in a very short time. She would have thought it more important for them to pace their mounts so the horses would last longer. But he knew best, she reasoned.

The bay Simon Ward was riding had been pushed so hard for the past two days that it gave signs of flagging. Simon spurred it on anyway. He was not about to slow the others down and have his wife fall into the clutches of the vile slavers a second time.

So overjoyed was Simon at finding Felicity that several more minutes went by before he awakened to the terrible mistake he had made. In his haste to save his wife, he had gone off and left the man who had been willing to risk all on their behalf. He had abandoned the one person he had met since leaving Boston whom he would rate as a true friend.

But the worst part, the thought that made Simon feel sick inside, was not that Nate King was all alone, nor that the trapper was as blind as the proverbial bat. No, what upset Simon the most was that it appeared the slavers were heading right for him.

Chapter Twelve

"Simon, wait!" Nate King called out as the Bostonian sped off into the night. It was useless. The younger man was not to be denied. Nate might as well try to stop a twister or a raging hailstorm. Love was as powerful a force as Nature itself; some would say it was more powerful.

The frontiersman poked the black stallion and set out to follow Ward. He wanted to keep Simon out of trouble, to be there in case he was needed. But he had not gone more than ten yards when the stallion suddenly dug in its front hooves and slid to a stop. A distinct rattling told him why. He cut to the right to keep the horse from being bitten just as the snake's rattles sounded again.

To Nate's consternation, the stallion reared. He made a grab for its neck, but he had been taken unawares. The next thing he knew, he was on his back on the ground and the big black was racing to the southwest. Nate went to rise but changed his mind on hearing the rattlesnake. It was so close that he could have reached out and picked it up.

Few city-bred folks were aware that rattlers liked to do most of their hunting at night. Fewer still knew that the deadly reptiles thrived on the plains. Small wonder, since the prairie was where prairie dog towns were found, and prairie dogs were a rattlesnake staple.

Nate King knew, of course. The knowledge afforded scant comfort as he lay there in the sweet-smelling grass listening to the brittle harbinger of impending death.

Nate did not twitch a muscle. He did not even blink. Any movement, however slight, might provoke the snake into striking. Rigid as a log, he prayed the reptile would wander elsewhere, and do it soon. But a minute went by. Two.

Then, to compound Nate's predicament, the black stallion's familiar whinny carried to him across the prairie. The stallion had recovered from its fright and was heading back.

Most other horses would have fled until exhaustion brought them to a stop. Not the big black. It was made of firmer stuff, yet another reason the trapper valued it so highly.

The rattling ceased. The grass close to Nate's arm rustled. The scrape of scales was loud enough for him to tell that the rattler was leaving. Moments later the stallion trotted up. Rising, he stepped toward it, one arm outstretched. As soon as he touched its sweaty side, he swung up.

The delay had proven costly. Simon was long gone. Nate listened and thought he heard hoofbeats. Taking it for granted that Simon's bay was the source, he headed out, riding slowly, a sitting duck if ever there had been one.

It troubled Nate to think that he might be wrong, that maybe he had gotten turned around when he fell and he was now going in the wrong direction. But it was a chance he had to take, for the Wards' sake.

The fall seemed to have had an unforeseen effect. Nate was gratified to note that he could now make out the motion of the stallion's head, although the horse was no more than a great fuzzy blur. To test himself, he held the Hawken within six inches of his face and moved the barrel back and forth. Again he could distinguish the motion, although the barrel itself was a dark smudge against the backdrop of night sky.

Encouraged, Nate ventured on. Given the time that had elapsed, he figured that Simon couldn't be more than half a mile ahead of him at the very most.

Then a shot rang out. Nate drew rein, puzzled. The retort came from off to the west, not the southeast, and it was much closer than he had assumed Simon would be. Had the younger man strayed off course? he wondered. That seemed highly unlikely, since Simon had the slaver camp fire to serve as a beacon. The only possible explanation was that he was the one who had strayed.

Nate promptly worked the reins and rode westward. He held the stallion to a brisk walk and bent at the waist with an ear cocked to the breeze. There might not be much warning when he ran into the slavers. He hung on every noise, no matter how faint.

So it was that Nate detected the sounds of a scuffle long before he might have done so otherwise. The loud grunt of a man was mixed with the rustling of grass. Dreading that Simon had been jumped by slavers, he hastened closer. A lusty bellow helped him pinpoint the exact spot.

"You're going to die, bitch! Do you hear me? I don't care what Gregor wants. You're mine!"

Nate stiffened. It had to be Mrs. Ward in the clutches of one of the cutthroats! He fingered the Hawken, his thumb on the hammer. The struggle grew louder. Again the man bellowed.

"Die, squaw! Die!"

So it wasn't Felicity Ward, Nate realized, relieved. He had no time to ponder the mystery, for moments later he heard the crackle of grass and a bestial growl only a few yards ahead. Instantly he reined up. By narrowing his eyes he could make out a vague pair of clenched figures. But he could not tell which was the woman and which was her assailant.

A choking sob prompted Nate to act before the woman was slain. Since he couldn't determine which one to shoot, he decided to try a bluff. Leveling the Hawken, he declared in a flinty tone, "That's enough! Get up with your hands in the air, mister! And be quick about it!"

Winona King had seen a rider appear out of the gloom. At first, she did not recognize him. Her lungs were close to bursting from lack of air; her vision danced in circles. Then, for a few heartbeats, it cleared. Winona was so astounded at seeing her mate that she went limp with shock, certain that she must be seeing things, that her eyes were deceiving her.

It was fitting, she mused, that in her final fevered moments of life she should imagine the man who had claimed her love was right there in front of her.

The vision spoke. The voice was her husband's, but he did not say the things she wanted to hear. He did not tell her that he cared and would go on caring forever. He did not say how much he would miss her, or how wrong it was that she had been snatched from him when they both were in the prime of their lives. Instead, her vision barked an order. And to her bewilderment, the slaver heard, too, because he let go of her as if her neck were a red hot ember and leaped to his feet.

But that could only mean one thing! Winona told herself. She propped her hands on the ground and attempted to sit up, but she was too weak, her mind too sluggish. She saw Simpson elevate his arms and her Nate cover him.

Something was wrong, though. Winona sensed it in the core of her being. And she was sure that whatever it was had to do with Nate.

In a rush, clarity returned. Winona started to rise. She noticed that Nate was holding the Hawken at the wrong angle, that the barrel pointed at her instead of the slaver. Simpson had noticed, also, because his left hand was slowly dipping toward his other flintlock. Strangely, Nate seemed not to realize it.

Winona could not call out a warning. Her throat was too raw. She could barely croak, let alone speak. Yet if she did not do something—and swiftly—she would lose her man. Planting both moccasins, she marshaled all the strength she had left and launched herself upward. Her right hand closed on the hilt of Simpson's long butcher knife as the slaver drew the pistol. He was extending the flintlock when the blade sank into his side below the ribs.

Simpson arched his spine, threw back his head, and opened his mouth as if to scream. No sound came out. He staggered a few steps. Winona kept pace, holding the knife in place. The slaver twisted his head to glare at her. "You lousy squaw! You've done kilt me!" So saying, his arm sagged and his whole body deflated as might a punctured water skin. He twitched for a bit once he curled onto the grass, then stopped breathing.

Nate had seen the blur of movement but had no idea what was going on until the man spoke. Filled with anxiety, he dismounted to help the woman. "Ma'am? Are you all right? I—"

The trapper never got to finish his statement. A warm form flew into his arms and suddenly words of ardent love and tender endearments were being whispered in his ear. The shock of recognition made his legs go weak. "Winona?" Her lips confirmed it and smothered his with tiny hot kisses. For the longest while after that they stood there in a quiet embrace.

Winona was the first to break the spell. Looking up, she said, "My heart sings with joy at seeing you again, husband. But how did you know the slavers had taken me captive?"

Briefly, Nate sketched his encounter with the Bostonian and the events since. Even as he talked, his vision cleared a little more. By the time he was done, he could make out her eyes, nose and mouth although they were not crystal-clear as yet. She reached up and brushed her fingertips over the skin below his eyes.

"You take too many risks, husband. Take no more until you can see again."

"I don't have much choice in the matter," Nate responded. "We have to help those greenhorns if we can." He stepped into the stirrups, lowered his arm to give her a boost, and wheeled the stallion. "Can you see any sign of a camp fire?"

"Yes," Winona said. "I will guide you."

Nate smiled as one of her arms looped around his

waist. It flabbergasted him that they were together again. By the same token, inwardly he quaked to think of the grisly fate that would have been her lot had he not stumbled on her at just the right moment. It was almost as if a higher power had a hand in her salvation.

Presently Nate could see the fire too. No voices came from the camp, which disturbed him. It was much too early for all the slavers to have turned in.

The night itself was much too tranquil, reminding Nate of the lull before a storm. He slowed to be on the safe side. Since he had given the Hawken to his wife, he drew a pistol.

"The camp is deserted except for four horses," Winona whispered. "We can go right on in."

"Unless it's a trap," Nate said. It made no sense for the slavers to have gone off and left their camp unattended. He stayed where he was for several minutes until convinced that it would be safe.

The tethered horses displayed no alarm. Nate rode to where packs, parfleches and a few saddles were piled near the crackling flames.

"It looks as if they left in a hurry," Winona commented, reading the tracks by the firelight. "Perhaps they are after your friend."

"And they took his wife along?" Nate shook his head. "They would have left her behind, under guard. No, I reckon Simon got her away from them somehow, and the whole kit and caboodle lit a shuck after him. See if you can tell which direction they went."

Winona slid off and walked to the edge of the clearing. She made a circuit of the perimeter, stooping every so often to examine the soil. Freshly overturned clods of dirt showed her exactly where the slavers had entered the grass. "Over here," she said.

Nate had been keeping an eye out for slavers. His vision was almost back to normal. A little while more and he would be able to give the renegades a taste of their own medicine.

Holding the pistol in his left hand, Nate rode toward his wife. It seemed to him that she had never been as lovely as she was at that exact moment, with the dancing firelight playing off her smooth features and the shadows at her back.

Then one of those shadows moved. Nate went to shout a warning, but the shadow pounced before he could. A brawny Indian in a breechcloth seized Winona from behind, pinned her arms to her sides, and started to drag her toward the grass. She resisted by digging in her heels and slamming her head backward.

Nate raised the flintlock and charged to her aid. He had to get a lot closer before he dared fire. Suddenly another figure popped up out of the grass, pointed a rifle at him, and fired. In the slaver's haste, the man missed. Nate swiveled, fixed as steady a bead as he could, held it, and stroked the trigger.

The cutthroat screeched as he flung his hands up and keeled over.

The black stallion was almost to the grass. Winona heard it coming. She knew that Nate would leap down to help her, and the thought filled her with dread. With his eyesight dimmed, he would be no match for the Lipan.

Fear lent added strength to Winona's limbs. She had tried to butt the Lipan in the face, but he always turned his cheek to her. She had tried kicking his legs out from under him, but he planted himself so firmly that an avalanche would not have budged him. Now Winona took a new tack. She still had the Hawken clutched in her right hand. Glancing down, she saw the Lipan's left foot next to her leg. Without hesitation she drove the stock down onto his toes.

Something cracked. The warrior took a hopping step backward, pulling her after him. Winona swung the rifle around behind the two of them and tried to snare his legs to trip him. She succeeded, but she could not hold on. The Hawken fell.

Nate saw all this as he vaulted from the stallion. He rushed to help her when yet another slaver reared up off to the right. Nate dropped as a rifle cracked. The ball whizzed overhead like a riled hummingbird. Straightening, Nate saw the slaver barrel toward him while unlimbering a pistol.

Somewhere, a gruff voice yelled, "Owens! Don't be a jackass! Stay down until we nail him!"

The onrushing slaver paid no heed.

The Hawken was only a few yards away, but Nate could not hope to reach it before Owens reached him. He needed to slow the man down for just a second or two. To that end, Nate pointed his spent pistol as if he were going to shoot.

Owens ducked and veered a few feet to one side.

Which was just what Nate wanted him to do. Taking a single long stride, Nate dived. He released the pistol in midair so he could scoop up the Hawken as he hit the ground. In a smooth roll he rose to his knees and leveled the rifle at his waist at the selfsame moment that the slaver crashed out of the grass right in front of him.

Owens had his pistol up, but as he burst into full view his attention was drawn to the fierce struggle between Chipota and Winona. Belatedly, he spied the crouched figure in the shadows in front of him.

At a range of no more than a yard, Nate fired. The Hawken boomed and kicked. The heavy caliber slug caught the slaver in the stomach and lifted him off his feet.

Owens was hurled back into the grass. He screamed as he crashed down. Rolling into a ball, he clutched the large hole in his gut and wailed in torment.

Nate moved in quickly, eager to help Winona. He drew his butcher knife as he stood over the squalling cutthroat. Owens glanced up, foresaw his impending doom, and uttered a high-pitched scream.

"*Noooooooooooo!*"

A short thrust silenced the wavering cry. Nate turned and saw the man's pistol lying on the ground. He picked it up, then ran toward his wife. More concerned for her welfare than his own, he almost missed spotting the grizzled slaver who swooped toward him.

Nate twisted, thereby saving his life. The newcomer already had a rifle pressed to a shoulder, and fired. The lead ball creased Nate's side, digging a shallow furrow low down on his ribs. It provoked an intense spasm of raw pain and drew blood, but it did not stop Nate from extending the pistol he had just snatched off the ground, curling back the hammer, and squeezing.

The slaver called Ricket had not lived as long as he had by being reckless. He truly thought that he had the big stranger dead to rights. He'd seen the man shoot Williams with the only pistol the man had on him. Then he'd seen Owens go down. Figuring that the stranger's guns were all empty, Ricket had closed in to do the job right.

The crack of the pistol was the last sound Earl Ricket ever heard.

While all this had been going on, Winona King had drawn the knife she had taken from Simpson and turned on the Lipan. She slashed at his torso as he grabbed at her neck. The blade sliced in smoothly but was deflected by a rib. Chipota grunted, seized her knife arm, and flung her to the ground.

As she came down, Winona kicked. She clipped the Lipan on the thigh. It was not a forceful blow, but it did prevent him from pouncing on her.

Chipota skirted to the left. His war club lay nearby but he did not retrieve it. Nor did he draw the knife at his hip. Evidently he planned to take her alive, or else he was going to throttle the life from her with his bare hands.

Winona was not about to submit to either. Swiveling on her back like an overturned turtle, she held him at bay with the point of the butcher knife. His bronzed hand flicked at her wrist. She parried and nearly took off a few fingers. An odd smile lit his face as he skipped to the right, tensed, and sprang.

Winona was a hair too slow. She winced when a rock-hard fist batted her arm aside and knees as stout as tree trunks rammed into her stomach. The stars swirled. Her knife was plucked from her fingers. She blinked and looked up. Chipota was on top of her, but he did not stay there.

A human battering ram clad in buckskins hurtled out of nowhere and slammed into the Lipan's chest. Both men catapulted into the grass. Winona sat up, her heart in her throat at the sight of the muscular warrior and her husband locked in mortal combat. Chipota had the knife raised to strike, but Nate held the warrior's arm back.

They rolled first one way, then another. Nate put all he had into pinning his foe so he could finish the warrior off, but the slaver twisted and shifted like a greased snake. For some reason it reminded Nate of the time he had fought an Apache down in New Mex-

David Thompson

ico. Why that should be, he didn't know.

Chipota was highly skilled at close-quarters combat. All the warriors in his tribe were. Like their Apache brethren, they lived for war, and had been doing so for so many generations that they had few equals.

Chipota, in particular, had always preferred to slay his enemies up close. It gave him pleasure to see the life fade from their eyes and feel their limbs grow weak. It was why he liked to use a war club instead of a bow or lance or gun.

The Lipan's passion for dispensing death was in part to blame for his being banished from the tribe. When another warrior had made light of him once too many times, he'd leaped on the man and strangled him right there in front of half the village.

Now Chipota intended to add to his long string of victims. Muscles rippling, he sought to bury his knife in the white-eye who had rashly attacked him. He did not expect much resistance since it had been his experience that whites, by and large, were weaklings. In his previous clashes with them, he had never so much as worked up a sweat.

This white-eye proved to be the exception. Chipota strained, but was met by equal strength. He tried to tear his arm free so he could stab but was held fast by a grip that rivaled his own. He resorted to every trick he knew in order to break the white-eye's hold but was balked at every turn.

Even as Chipota fought, in the back of his mind he wondered about the white man's identity. When he had come on the pair shortly after finding Simpson's body, he had assumed the white man to be a stray trapper. But while trailing them to the camp, the warrior had seen how the Shoshone pressed herself against the white-eye, how she held him and touched him. She would not do that to just any man. No, not her.

It had to be the woman's mate, Chipota had concluded. The Shoshone had been telling them all along that her man would come to free her. The white slavers had laughed at her, having heard many women make the same claim in the past.

For once, their captive had been telling the truth.

Now Chipota was fighting for his life against an adversary every bit as formidable as any he had ever faced. As they continued to grapple, he drove a knee at the white-eye's groin.

The Shoshone's husband blocked it by shifting so that his hip absorbed the blow. Then the white-eye pivoted, hooked a leg behind Chipota's, and flipped the Lipan onto his back.

Rather abruptly, Chipota found himself staring up at the tip of his own knife as it was forced inexorably downward toward his throat. He exerted every ounce of strength he had to keep the blade from penetrating his flesh, but it was not enough.

The wily warrior worked his legs to the right and managed to bend them at the knees. All he had to do was sweep his feet up and around and he would dislodge the white-eye. But as he coiled to do so, the unexpected occurred. Hands took hold of his ankles and yanked his legs straight. Before he quite comprehended what was going on, someone sat on his shins. In desperation he attempted to tug loose, but the weight pinned his legs in place.

Insight brought a rare smile of resignation to the Lipan's lips. It was over. He had done his best but it was not good enough, not against the both of them. As the butcher knife slowly sheared into his jugular, he regretted that he had not met the Shoshone many winters ago when they were both young. It would have been nice to make her into his woman—whether she wanted to be it or not.

Nate King gave a final wrench. The blade sank to the hilt. He stayed on top of the warrior, blood splattering him on the cheeks and chin, until a hand tapped him on the shoulder.

"It is over, husband. He is dead."

Straightening, Nate slid his damp hand off the slick hilt. He was taken aback to find his wife perched on the warrior's shins. His other hand covered her knee as he surveyed the bodies lying nearby.

"I'm afraid it's not over yet. We still have to find the Wards."

At that very moment, Simon and Felicity Ward and their Mexican ally were fleeing for their lives. Julio was in the lead. Simon and his wife rode abreast of one another. Ahead of them lay countless miles of swaying grass. Behind them, hot on their trail, were Gregor and the band of cutthroats.

It had all gone so well there for a while. Simon had been convinced that they had given the slavers the slip. Then he had remembered Nate King, alone and defenseless, and he had turned the bay while yelling for the others to go on.

What possessed him to think they'd obey, Simon would never know. Almost immediately Felicity had wheeled to follow him, so of course Julio had done the same. Simon had reined up and gestured for them to turn around but they ignored him.

"Where are you going?" Felicity had demanded.

"The man who helped me find you is in trouble. I have to go help him," Simon had quickly explained. "The two of you should go on. We'll catch up by daylight, I would imagine."

Felicity looked at him as if he were insane. "You

can't be serious. After all we've been through, do you really think I would stand for being separated again? Where you go, dearest, I go."

Simon had appealed to Julio. "Talk some sense into her. You know what will happen if the slavers get their hands on us. She has to go with you."

To the young man's annoyance, the Mexican had said, "So sorry, senor, but this is between the two of you. I will abide by whatever you two decide."

"Then it's settled. We'll search for your friend," Felicity declared, and made as if to ride back the way they had come.

"No!" Simon had objected, barring her path. "I want you out of here, now! Get to safety and don't fret about me!"

A retort had been on the tip of Felicity's tongue. But it was never voiced. For from out of the night to the west rose a cry of triumph.

"Did you hear that, boys? We're closer than we thought. After the bastards!"

It had been Gregor. The slavers had thundered toward them with yips and howls. Simon had no choice but to forget about the mountain man for the time being.

That had been half an hour ago. All three of their horses now showed signs of fatigue. Simon knew it was just a matter of time before they had to make a stand, and he was not about to delude himself over the outcome. Even with Julio's help, it was preordained.

A minor godsend of sorts in the shape of a low knoll rose before them. Julio raced to the top, hauled on his reins, and was out of the saddle before his animal stopped moving. Rushing a few yards down the slope, he knelt and aimed his rifle.

Simon was only a few steps behind. He tucked his

rifle to his shoulder as a ragged cluster of slavers materialized, bearing down on the knoll like a pack of frenzied Cossacks.

The cutthroats had not expected their quarry to turn. Gregor was the first to spot the kneeling figures and bellowed, "Scatter! We're in their sights!" Suiting action to words, he swung onto the off side of his mount, Indian fashion, and angled to the north. Some of the others did the same.

Julio and Simon fired at the same moment. Two of the slavers were knocked from their mounts, never to rise again. A third was downed by Julio, who drew one of his fancy pistols in a blur and banged off the shot just as the rider was about to shoot the Bostonian. Simon whipped out his own pistol, but by then the slavers had scattered into the high grass.

"We must ride, senor, before they think to cut us off," the Mexican urged.

Nodding, Simon started back up the knoll. Felicity had climbed down and held the reins of all three animals. He had almost reached her when several shots rang out. One struck Trijillo's mount in the neck. The horse whinnied and reared, throwing the bay and Felicity's animal into a panic. She tried to hold on, but several more shots were all it took to send the three horses racing off in different directions.

Julio made a frantic bid to catch his. He chased it partway down the far side and only stopped when another rifle cracked and a ball cored his right thigh.

Simon saw their newfound friend jerk to the impact and fall. He sprinted to Julio's side. Propping an arm under the Mexican's shoulder, Simon began to haul him to the top when to his dismay Felicity appeared on the other side of Julio to take his other arm. "Get down in the grass," Simon directed. "They can't hit what they can't see."

"He helped me when I needed it."

And that was all she would say. They regained the crown without another shot being fired. Sinking low, Simon eased Julio onto his back. The thigh was bleeding badly and Trijillo had his teeth clenched. "Hang on," Simon said. "I'll cut my shirt to make a tourniquet."

"No time, senor!" Julio said, clutching Simon's wrist. "They will come soon. They will wipe us out."

Simon did it anyway. There had been a time not all that long ago when he would have broken down in tears at the setback they had suffered. He would have been devastated. But that was the old Simon Ward. This was the new. He calmly accepted the inevitable. Sliding his knife from its leather sheath, he shrugged out of his shirt and bent to his task.

Felicity had her head turned into the wind. "They're moving around down there," she reported. "I can hear a lot of whispering. They must be up to something."

"They are surrounding us," Julio said. "There is no way out now. I am sorry, senora."

"For what? Trying to save my life?" Felicity took his hand in hers. "Be still now. You'll only make the bleeding worse."

The next 15 minutes were the worst of Simon's whole life. Not because he knew that in a very short while he would die, but because of what he had to do when the slavers overran them. He glanced at his wife and prayed he would find the courage.

Julio insisted on sitting up after he was bandaged. He reloaded his guns and gave one of his expensive pistols to Felicity.

The rustling and whispering stopped, but it was not quiet for long. To the north, Gregor bellowed,

"The jig is up, Ward. I don't know how you survived being shot, but it doesn't hardly matter. Your wife is ours whether you like it or not. So make it easy on yourself and turn her over to us, pronto."

The words seemed to rise from Simon's throat of their own accord. "Go to hell, you son of a bitch! You'll never get your hands on her again!"

"That's what you think!"

A pistol cracked. Simon ducked, thinking he was the target, but the shot was only the signal for all the slavers to rise up at once and rush the knoll. He fired his rifle and one dropped, fired his pistol and a second toppled. Beside him Julio brought down two more. Felicity's pistol banged, but Simon did not see whether she hit anyone.

The onrushing line slowed but did not break. Slavers cut loose all around the knoll. Felicity gasped as a burning sensation seared her arm. She heard a bullet thud into Julio, as did a second, and a third.

Both men reloaded frantically. Simon had his rifle primed but not the pistol when several slavers loomed in front of him. He planted a ball in the forehead of the foremost. Julio's pistol took an added toll.

Then their guns were empty and the slavers were on them. Simon streaked out his knife and pivoted to plunge it into Felicity as he had promised himself he would do. He froze.

Gregor was a few feet away. The giant slaver had the barrel of his rifle centered on Simon's head. "You should have listened, boy!"

Simon would never forget the sight of the top of Gregor's head exploding in a shower of brains and gore. He thought that Julio had fired, but when he glanced around he discovered their friend was on the ground, riddled with holes.

The answer came in the form of two riders who tore into the startled slavers as if they were chaff before a storm. In savage fury the pair slew cutthroats right and left. Many of the slavers had emptied their guns and had not had time to reload. They were easy prey.

Six slavers fell in twice as many seconds, and then the man sprang from his black stallion and was among them, wielding a butcher knife. Three more lay wheezing in puddles of their own blood before the few who lived fled down the knoll and vanished in the grass.

Just like that, it was over.

Felicity Ward turned from the mound of earth at the top of the knoll and walked with bowed head to her horse. She looked at the others. "He saved my life and I never even knew his real name."

Nate King patted a parfleche tied behind his saddle. "I'll take his possibles to Bent's Fort. There's a letter, written in Spanish. I think it's to his folks. William Bent will see that everything goes south on the next wagon train to Santa Fe. From there, it can be sent to his family. They'll learn what he did. I expect they'll be right proud."

"I hope so," Felicity said sincerely.

Nate faced the younger man. "What about the two of you? What have you decided?"

Simon exchanged glances with his wife. "We talked it over most of the night and all of this morning. You'll probably think we're out of our minds, but we want to stick it out. We can't let all that has happened be for nothing."

"Well, I'll be," Nate said, genuinely surprised. "Whereabouts do you want to settle?"

"We were hoping you could help us out in that regard."

Winona King laughed. "I have always wanted neighbors. How would you like to live in the next valley over from ours? There is plenty of water and game. And I would have someone to visit with when my husband is gone weeks at a time trapping."

"Oh, could we?" Felicity beamed, clapping her hands.

Simon was just as delighted. "This means that Nate can teach me all I need to know about surviving in the wilderness. Let's get going! I can hardly wait to see this valley." Prodding the bay, he took the lead, but he had only gone a few feet when the trapper called his name. "What is it?" he asked, reining up.

"Your first lesson. You're going in the wrong direction."

#45
WILDERNESS
IN CRUEL CLUTCHES
David Thompson

Zach King, son of legendary mountain man Nate King, is at home in the harshest terrain of the Rockies. But nothing can prepare him for the perils of civilization. Locked in a deadly game of cat-and-mouse with his sister's kidnapper, Zach wends his way through the streets of New Orleans like the seasoned hunter he is. Yet this is not the wild, and the trappings of society offer his prey only more places to hide. Dodging fists, knives, bullets and even jail, Zach will have to adjust to his new territory quickly—his sister's life depends on it.

MAX BRAND®

JOKERS EXTRA WILD

Anyone making a living on the rough frontier took a bit of a gamble, but no Western writer knows how to up the ante like Max Brand. In "Speedy—Deputy," the title character racks up big winnings on the roulette wheel, but that won't help him when he's named deputy sheriff—a job where no one's lasted more than a week. "Satan's Gun Rider" continues the adventures of the infamous Sleeper, whose name belies his ability to bury a knife to the hilt with just a flick of his wrist. And in the title story, a professional gambler inherits a ring that lands him in a world of trouble.

PETER DAWSON

FORGOTTEN DESTINY

Over the decades, Peter Dawson has become well known for his classic style and action-packed stories. This volume collects in paperback for the first time three of his most popular novellas—all of which embody the dramatic struggles that made the American frontier unique and its people the stuff of legends. The title story finds Bill Duncan on the way to help his friend Tom Bostwick avoid foreclosure. But along the trail, Bill's shot, robbed and left for dead—with no memory of who he is or where he was going. Only Tom can help him, but a crooked sheriff plans to use Bill as a pawn to get the Bostwick spread for himself. Can Bill remember whose side he's supposed to be on before it's too late?

- -

Dorchester Publishing Co., Inc.
P.O. Box 6640 _____5548-1
Wayne, PA 19087-8640 $5.99 US/$7.99 CAN

Please add $2.50 for shipping and handling for the first book and $.75 for each additional book. NY and PA residents, add appropriate sales tax. No cash, stamps, or CODs. Canadian orders require an extra $2.00 for shipping and handling and must be paid in U.S. dollars. Prices and availability subject to change. **Payment must accompany all orders.**

Name: _____

Address: _____

City: _____ State: _____ Zip: _____

E-mail: _____

I have enclosed $_____ in payment for the checked book(s).

CHECK OUT OUR WEBSITE! www.dorchesterpub.com
_____ Please send me a free catalog.

LOREN ZANE GREY

AMBUSH FOR LASSITER

Framed for a murder they didn't commit, Lassiter and his best pal Borling are looking at twenty-five years of hard time in the most notorious prison of the West. In a daring move, they make a break for freedom—only to be double-crossed at the last minute. Lassiter ends up in solitary confinement, but Borling takes a bullet to the back. When at last Lassiter makes it out, there's only one thing on his mind: vengeance.

RIDERS TO MOON ROCK

ANDREW J. FENADY

Like the stony peak of Moon Rock, Shannon knew what it was to be beaten by the elements yet stand tall and proud despite numerous storms. Shannon never quite fit in with the rest of the world. First raised by Kiowas and then taken in by a wealthy rancher, he found himself rejected by society time after time. Everything he ever wanted was always just out of his grasp, kept away by those who resented his upbringing and feared his ambition. But Shannon is determined to wait out his enemies and take what is rightfully his—no matter what the cost.